Tales Ridiculous and Sublime

Tales Ridiculous
and Sublime
....

*To Our dear Heather & Stuart
With my warmest wishes
Cyril   APRIL 2011*

Cyril Smith

Copyright © 2011 by Cyril Smith.

Library of Congress Control Number: 2011903191
ISBN: Hardcover 978-1-4568-6807-9
Softcover 978-1-4568-6806-2
Ebook 978-1-4568-6808-6

All rights reserved. No part of this book may be reproduced or transmitted in any form or by any means, electronic or mechanical, including photocopying, recording, or by any information storage and retrieval system, without permission in writing from the copyright owner.

This is a work of fiction. Names, characters, places and incidents either are the product of the author's imagination or are used fictitiously, and any resemblance to any actual persons, living or dead, events, or locales is entirely coincidental.

This book was printed in the United States of America.

To order additional copies of this book, contact:
Xlibris Corporation
0-800-644-6988
www.xlibrispublishing.co.uk
Orders@xlibrispublishing.co.uk

The Author, C.N. SMITH, was born into a military family overseas where his father was serving at the time. He was orphaned at an early age and educated in a military boarding school. He, like his father, became a regular soldier. His army career began in The **R**oyal **E**lectrical and **M**echanical **E**ngineers, as an electrician, and he was with them when he served in Korea from the start of the war there. Later he transferred to the 3rd Carabiniers, a cavalry (tanks) regiment and served in other theatres of trouble, including Kenya, Suez, Cyprus, Aden and Kuwait.

At the end of his army career he joined the Civil Service where he worked until he reached retirement age.

He is also the author of **CHRISTMAS TALES**, his first series of short stories, sold in aid of charity.

Now, a septuagenarian, he spends his time writing stories with the intention to help others in society.

Acknowledgements

Publication of this series of TALES would not have been possible without the help of all those involved at **Xlibris**.

My grateful thanks go to **Nigel Ham** who read 'JAKE' and asked if he could explain what really happened to Jake in order to help other pet owners who could find themselves confronted with such a situation. The explanation, in the Epilogue written by Nigel, is at the end of the story. Also to **Caron and Steve Trees** who, after reading the first series of TALES, have encouraged me to keep on writing—hence this second series—and last but not least to my wife, **Patricia**.

Titles of Tales in this Series

Ginger 13

Jake 21

Epilogue from Nigel 32

Trade Secret 36

The Happy One 48

The Wedding 61

Hammer & Sickle 70

The Refuse Man 82

Sherlock Homes 91

The Reverend 103

Ginger

Dedicated to Steve Trees "a twitcher"

George "Ginger" Beer now lives in a ground floor maisonette with a rather large back yard that tries to resemble a garden. In one corner at the back of the yard is small disused bike shed next to which is a dog's kennel, left there by the previous occupants of the maisonette. Ginger lives alone. This is not unusual for a twenty four year old. However, he does have two companions.

Just prior to leaving his last dwelling an American acquaintance offered Ginger a parrot that he had brought over from Louisiana, a southern state of the United States. The acquaintance was returning home to America and his beloved Dixieland and did not feel that the parrot was worth the palaver involved in order to take him back there. This was also due to the fact that the parrot irritated him with his raucous voice, and its brilliant mimicry of the human voice in speech and song. It was also a naughty parrot that became quite an annoyance, as Ginger would find out in due course. The American did not tell Ginger the parrot's name so on getting him settled in his cage at home Ginger asked the parrot what he was called. Instead of just telling Ginger his name the parrot burst out singing one of the old music hall songs:

I'm 'enery the eighth I am
'enery the eighth I am, I am.
I'm married to the girl next door,
She's been married seven times before.
And every one was an 'enery,
There never was a Billy or a Sam,
I'm the eighth one called old 'enery
'enery the eighth I am.

"Oh! That's very good!" responded Ginger. "So your name is Henry. Well, my name is George but everyone calls me Ginger because my surname is Beer. Do you understand?"

"I do, I do", replied the parrot. "Listen Ginger, when do I get some food and, if you let me out of my cage to fly around the room, I promise I won't fly away", said 'enery in his harsh high-pitched voice. Ginger soon heated some baked beans on toast for himself and the parrot. They both enjoyed it but Ginger was astonished at the fluency of speech from 'enery. It's a wonder he did not have a Dixieland accent!

Ginger had recently started a new job with a small firm of builders who were currently renovating a house near to where he lived. Rather a posh house with a large back garden and a swimming pool filled with water that was turning brackish. He was not used to working in the building trade and had quite a lot to learn but nevertheless he was earning money doing all the odd jobs.

The foreman, Jack Dempsey, approached Ginger and said, "I'm off to the Builders' Merchant to get a few bits and pieces and then I am calling at the office to check some paperwork. Whilst I'm away, you see that door over there—pointing to a door leaning against the wall—could you hang it for me. If you need a hand, Steve, who is shovelling rubble into a skip in the front garden, will help you, alright?"

"Okay governor, I'll do that. You want it hanged in that gap there?"

"Yea, hang it there", replied Jack, without looking in the direction to which Ginger was pointing, and then trotted off.

When the foreman returned he immediately went over to Ginger and asked him curiously, "what happened to the door—where is it?"

"I threw it into the swimming pool governor", rather astounded that Jack had asked.

"What did you do that for you b—idiot?"

"Well gov' it was much easier drowning it than hanging it—I couldn't find any rope", replied Ginger.

"Well, well, well—I've heard it all now. Yesterday I asked you to put some of that rubble in the wheelbarrow, run it up the plank and dump it into the skip. What did you do? You dumped the barrow into the skip as well and we had a hell of a job getting it out. What did you do in your last job—sitting in front of a computer I suppose?"

"No gov', I was a sprayer", answered Ginger.

"A sprayer—what, spraying cars or other vehicles, or spraying roses and shrubs with aphid repellent all over gardens and so on?"

"Kangaroo repellent gov'."

"But we do not have kangaroos in Buckinghamshire."

"That is because I used to spray kangaroo repellent all over the place", replied Ginger.

"Well boy, I think you should go and see a doctor or a head psychiatrist as there is something wrong with you in my humble opinion. Now go and retrieve that door from the swimming pool and lean it back against the wall to dry out!" Jack then stormed off rather angrily.

Ginger had been to see the doctor the previous week but it was a fruitless visit. After waiting well over an hour in the reception area he approached the receptionist and asked whether there were five volumes of "*The Decline and fall of the Roman Empire*" by Edward Gibbon, at the reception desk, so that he could read them to pass away the waiting time. Sadly there was not so he asked if he could have a quick enema instead to kill time—again, sadly, no way! When he eventually saw Dr. Sean Flahity he settled comfortably in the chair near to the doctor. Dr. Sean was a dour Irishman.

"What can I do for you?" asked the doctor.

"I don't know", replied Ginger.

"Are you well?" asked the doctor.

"I'm fine", said Ginger—but when I saw you a month ago you said I was suffering from terminal dandruff and that you wanted to see me in a month—so here I am.

"I see", said the doctor. He immediately swung his chair around to face his computer monitor screen and tapped into Ginger's medical record. "There is no record here of my having seen you but tell me, did I prescribe anything for your terminal dandruff complaint?"

"Yes you did—you advised me to use Brylcreem—and you said it would clear up in about twenty years", replied Ginger.

"Oh! well please continue the treatment and we'll see how it goes—you can go now".

"Thank you doctor", Ginger said before leaving the room. He was immensely glad that he had not been given a prescription because, the last time he had visited the pharmacy, he waited so long to have his prescription dealt with that when he eventually got home and looked in the mirror he was not surprised to see that he had grown whiskers on his face due to the length of time he had been waiting.

* * *

About three weeks earlier some kind stranger had offered Ginger, and he accepted, a piglet as a pet. As he had a large enough yard and a kennel he felt he would have no trouble looking after it. Piggy was able to live and thrive on Ginger's food leftovers and was allowed the run of the house. Piggy was even keen on occasions to try and scrounge one of Ginger's roll up cigarettes.

"No, you can't have one—it will stunt your growth and you will not grow into a nice porkie", Ginger admonished him.

Ginger arrived home from work and, as it was Friday, he had the weekend to look forward to. Before settling down he rolled a cigarette and began smoking it. Henry, the parrot, spotted this and in a croaking voice rang out with the following song:

> *There's no smoking tonight,*
> *The moon is shining bright,*
> *And the stars are twinkling in the sky,*
> *Someone's a-watching us,*
> *Watching you and I,*
> *So let's go behind the bike shed*
> *And have a fag on the sly.*
> (Poet/lyricist not known)

"Shut up you noisy blighter, shut up!" shouted Ginger. Ginger then stood up to get a drink, scratching his posterior. The observant Henry noticed this and again piped up:

The Chinese detective, Charlie Chan, said to his number one son, *"Confucius—he say—**He who has itchy bum will have smelly finger.*"* (*Charlie Chan film series with a friend's quotation added*)

"Again, I say shut up or I'll wring your neck", warned Ginger.

Feeling rather dejected, because he was only having a laugh, Henry decided, in order to cheer himself up, he would sing again and burst forth with an old song much sung by troops years ago.

> *Oh! I put my finger up a woodpecker's h'le*
> *And the woodpecker said,* **"God Bless My Soul**
> **Take it out—take it out—take it out—take it out."**
> *So, I took my finger from the woodpecker's h'le and the woodpecker*
> *said,* **"God Bless My Soul, put it back, put it back, put it**
> **back, put it back".**
> *I wish I were in Dixie, OLAY-OLAY!*
> *In Dixieland I want to be where all the girls are pretty,*
> *OLAY-OLAY, I wish I were in Dixie!*

"You'll get Dixie in a minute if you don't shut up", Ginger retorted.

Ginger picked up a sealed bottle of mineral water and quite subconsciously read the label and cast his eyes over the DIRECTIONS FOR USE: Unscrew and remove cap.

> Pour contents into a glass.
> Replace the cap if bottle is not empty.
> Drink water.

"Well I wouldn't have known that. (As *Michael Caine* would say, *"not a lot of people know that"*).

The remainder of Saturday, after he had been shopping for provisions, Ginger felt very irate. The parrot irritated him by flying around the room leaving his droppings all over the furniture. In addition, piggy kept running in and out of the room from the back yard and he too left a couple of his droppings on the floor. Fed up to the hilt of cleaning up after the pair Ginger decided to deal with their messy behaviour once and for all. He grabbed piggy and dragged him, squealing, into the yard. Henry heard the commotion and the frightened squeals from piggy.

"Aha", he thought, "that's it—Ginger had cut his throat—poor little piggy".

Ginger came back into the room minus piggy. He seemed to have been silenced. Unbeknown to Henry, Ginger had locked piggy in the dog's kennel.

"Now it's your turn", Ginger said angrily to Henry. After many attempts he eventually caught Henry. He carried Henry into the kitchen to find a candle. Having found a candle he returned to the sitting room clutching the parrot and the candle. He sat on the settee, turned Henry on his back and on his lap and proceeded to light the candle. He then dropped, very accurately, the molten candle wax over Henry's rear end amidst screams from Henry. When the wax had set Ginger took Henry and shoved him back in his cage and locked the door. Henry was still screaming.

"That will show the pair of you that I mean business—messing all over my room. Now be quiet and go to sleep", shouted Ginger. That evening Ginger cleaned up all the mess in the room and went to bed.

Sunday morning, whilst still locked in his cage, Henry knew there was activity in the kitchen. Ginger was preparing his Sunday lunch. When it was all cooked and ready to eat Ginger carried his lunch, on a large tray, into the sitting room. Henry spotted a lump of roasted pork and stuffing on the plate and began to cry.

"OOOOH—poor piggy", he sobbed, poor-poor piggy and tearfully burst into verse.

Poor little suckling pig
Poor little swine
Sage and onion up your b-m
And candle wax up mine.

When he had finished eating his lunch Ginger washed up his cooking utensils, etc., and put them away. He regretted having been so harsh with Henry and piggy but he had to teach them to respect his home. He then took Henry out of his cage and gently removed the candle wax, cleaned Henry's cage and put him back into it. Next he went into the yard and released piggy from the dog kennel and told him to use the corner of the yard set aside for him to use as a toilet.

BOTH PETS BEHAVED THEMSELVES THEREAFTER!

THE END

Jake

This story is dedicated to **Nigel and Jake**. All the events and the odd characters are purely fictitious and imaginary, except the last event that is real and extant. The author hopes Nigel will not object to his and Jake's names being used or the poignant details of their current situation being put into print.

Jake is a handsome Belgian, short tan-haired shepherd dog and a pet to Nigel since he was a puppy. Nigel lives alone and quite happily shares his time at home with Jake in his two up and one down terraced house. Both have a deep understanding of each other and Jake loves his games with his pal Nigel in the back garden. Sadly, the full activity of these games is now very much restricted.

Jake loves his daily walks along the avenues leading to a well maintained nearby field where a long pathway skirts around small copses of a variety of trees. Nigel and Jake thoroughly enjoy the beauty of the cherry trees when in blossom in springtime and the magnificence of the changing colour of the leaves in autumn when, at both times of the year, the trees are a sight for sore eyes. The air is invigorating and both enjoy a hearty breakfast and supper, after their walks, when they return home. Devotion to each other is too tame a phrase to use to describe their relationship.

One evening in mid-February, when it was dark, on their return from a walk, there was a heavy frost settling early on the paving stones. Nigel quite accidentally slipped and fell on to his back and, when he tried to move, found that he could not get up. Jake, realising what had happened started sniffing around Nigel's head and giving him big licks in the hope that it would help him back on to his feet. Alas, it was not to be because after trying again, Nigel could not move to a sitting position or get back on to his feet.

"I'll be alright Jake in a little while if I lay back and rest", he told Jake. Several minutes later Nigel was still unable, through his fall, to move. The cold paving was beginning to have an effect on Nigel as it was gradually penetrating all parts of his body. Jake could not do anything as he was still attached to a lead being clutched by Nigel. Jake instinctively knew that he had to summon help. The only way he could do this was by barking. His loud barking continued for over twenty minutes before being investigated by a nearby neighbour who cautiously emerged from his house. As soon as he discovered the reason why the dog was barking he helped Nigel back onto his feet and helped him to limp slowly back to Nigel's home. The kindly neighbour realized that Nigel needed professional medical attention so he 'phoned for an ambulance to take Nigel to hospital. Jake was left at home—no supper, not that he would have eaten it in the circumstances. Nigel left hospital, some time later, with his broken ankle heavily encased in plaster of Paris. He was given a pair of crutches and taken home by ambulance.

After the neighbour had made a pot of tea for Nigel and was sure he could manage on his own, Nigel called Jake to come and sit beside him. "You are a wonderful pal. Your barking rescued me and saved me from agonizing pain and hypothermia—thank you", said Nigel whilst patting and hugging Jake. "I'll reward you—I promise".

It was late March when Nigel had his plaster cast removed and it was now time to reward Jake for his good deed on the night of his accident. He knew Jake, from two previous experiences, thoroughly enjoyed a trip to the seaside so he decided they would have a short three-day break at a seaside resort. They had been to the south coast previously so Nigel wanted to try the east coast. That evening he grabbed a 'phone book and tried boarding houses in Skegness, Great Yarmouth, Felixstowe and Southend. Unfortunately not one of the boarding houses had any vacancies where dogs were welcome. Nigel then tried Walton-on-the-Naze. Eureka! He found a reasonably priced boarding house that would accommodate owners with their dogs, provided the animals were house trained and behaved properly. Nigel snapped up the offer and paid the deposit by credit card.

They arrived at the boarding house and were soon settled in. Both the landlady and her husband were immediately attracted to Jake and expressed their thoughts that he was a wonderful, playful and friendly creature. After a quick lunch of fish and chips from the local chippy—Jake loved fish but was not keen on mushy peas—they both made their way to the beach even though the sky was cloudy and looked rather ominous. On arrival Nigel released Jake from his lead and the latter immediately ran down to the water's edge. He put his front paws into the seawater but quickly withdrew from the sea, as it was far too cold to have a swim. Jake suddenly spotted something and immediately bounded up the beach, despite Nigel calling to him to come back. Jake then disappeared out of sight but Nigel was sure he would return and sat down on the sand to wait for him. In his excitement at being somewhere different he sniffed all shrubs and crooks and crannies. Nigel waited and waited patiently for Jake to return although, as darkness fell he became very anxious and decided to follow up the beach calling out to Jake every so often but there was no response. Nigel thought that perhaps Jake had returned to the boarding house so he made his way back there but was upset and very worried to find that there had been no sign of Jake.

Nigel gave the landlady his mobile 'phone number in case there was a development and set off on foot through the small town in search of Jake. It was a fruitless exercise. Over the next two days Nigel searched for Jake, reported him missing to the local police and local RSPCA office and leaving with them his full contact details. Unfortunately there was no sign of Jake. It seemed that both Nigel and Jake were searching for one another and going around in circles but never meeting up.

On the third day Nigel had to vacate his lodgings by mid-day and return home to Aylesbury but, unfortunately, without Jake. Nigel was very depressed and extremely worried but he needed to return home because he had to return to work. He could not afford to lose his job and was not a skiver so would not go to the extent of pretending to be sick. After notifying the local police and local RSPCA Nigel set off with Jake's basket, lead and remaining cans of dog food, for home. He arrived home after the long drive back wondering all the time where on earth Jake could have gone. Home seemed so desolate without his beloved Jake. Nigel was absolutely at his wits end and felt dejected and lost. He had done everything he could to find Jake but, alas, without success.

Meanwhile, Jake was in dire straits because he could not find his master and friend. Several times he returned to the boarding house and barked outside the front gate that was closed, and too high to jump over, to no avail. There was only one option left to him—he had to return to his home in Aylesbury but where was he to begin. His instinct told him to use his sense of smell and as soon as he picked up the scent he made his way to the Naze railway station. Sneaking through the metal main gate he ran to the far end of the platform and waited. He was starving and thirsty because he had lived on scraps of food dropped by litter louts and the odd scraps from wheelie bins—the bins that had been pulled over by urban foxes—and to quench his thirst he had lapped up water from puddles when he came across one. It was not nice food and the water was muddy. He missed his scrumptious food and clean water Nigel always served up for him.

After waiting some time, a goods train trundled slowly along the railway track and through the station. It seemed to have come straight from the

Naze fiddle yard—so called because in the days when the railways were being established the early goods yard looked like a violin when seen with a bird's eye view of the area. That is, it had two parallel tracks converging into one outward and one inward track with storage and loading bays alongside the tracks. Hence those who worked (and thieved) at the goods yard were said to be 'on the fiddle'. Jake's opportunity had arrived. He leapt onto an empty five plank open truck and sat in the corner. His ears pricked up when he heard a man say, rather loudly, to the diesel locomotive driver,

"I'll see you again at Liverpool Street station mate".

Jake's instinct told him that he was heading in the right direction. Some eighteen hours later the goods train arrived at Liverpool Street and Jake bounded off through the concourse of the goods area and on to the London streets, busy with traffic of all descriptions. Jake was famished and thirsty although he had managed to slake his thirst by drinking from a rainwater puddle in the road. He was also able to forage again stale food from litterbins.

Jake spent many days and nights wandering through the streets of London, eating, drinking and sleeping whenever and wherever the opportunity arose. He was even captured by wardens—traffic wardens—not dog wardens on at least four occasions but each time he was able to escape the clutches of his captors. Through pure instinct he approached St. Marylebone station and found his way on to the concourse and on to a platform where there was a four-carriage train parked. The doors were open and passengers were boarding the train. Jake joined them not knowing in which direction the train was bound. He found a vacant spot under a seat and made himself comfortable. He had no idea whether or not the train was heading in the direction of Aylesbury but he was hoping its destination would be Aylesbury. Alas, it was not so and, after several stops, he realized the train had arrived at its destination when all the passengers had alighted from the carriage. Jake jumped off the train before the doors closed and found he was at Tring in

Hertfordshire, several miles from Aylesbury but his sense of smell told him that he was heading in the right direction. It was almost three weeks since he went astray from his master—through his own inquisitive nature sniffing out new and exciting new smells. He would never do it again!

Jake headed along the A41 towards Aston Clinton, running and walking, mostly in the drizzling rain until he eventually reached Weston Turville. From there it was a matter of time—four days from Tring—before he reached the main entrance to Stoke Mandeville Hospital. Although it was dark and the road lights were on he knew he was nearly home.

The dismal wet night caused Nigel to go to bed. He washed, donned his pyjamas went into the bedroom, closed the window and got into bed. He was about to go off to sleep when he heard loud barking coming from outside the house. The barking persisted for several minutes before Nigel threw on his dressing gown and went downstairs to investigate as the barking was beginning to sound desperate. He opened the door and like a flash of lightening Jake bounded into the room. He was dishevelled and very thin. He bounded up to Nigel, put his front paws on to Nigel's shoulders, whining, yapping, in between licking Nigel's face, with his tail wagging like a fiddlers elbow. He could not stop giving Nigel big licks. Jake was so happy to be home at last after his horrible adventure.

Nigel was so relieved and happy to see his dear Jake. He hugged him—asked him, "where have you been boy all this time—tell me? Did someone bring you back?" Nigel went outdoors to see if anyone was around but the road was silent and deserted. Jake's only identification was his tag on his collar with his name and Nigel's landline telephone number engraved on it. Nigel pondered the question and concluded that if some kind persons had brought him home they would have knocked on the door and made their introductions to him. Besides in order to find where to return Jake the person or persons would have 'phoned first to get the address. No, Jake had arrived home by instinct and unaided.

Nigel wondered and wished Jake could tell him and whilst stroking and hugging him he asked, "How did you get home boy".

Jake thought, "I had better to remain silent and be thought a fool than to speak out and remove all doubt". Jake knew he was no fool but it would be difficult to make Nigel understand.

"Never mine old lad—let's get you cleaned up before I give you something good to eat and drink. You've lost a lot of weight. I should think you've run all the way back home. Nigel filled Jake's bath, shampooed him and with the shower hose thoroughly rinsed all the soapsuds off, towel-dried him then dried his coat with the hair-dryer.

Unfortunately Nigel had given Jake's tins of dog food and biscuits to another dog owner because the food would go stale if kept too long. However, he had one of Jake's favourites in the cupboard—a tin of corned beef. He mixed the chunks of beef with broken cream cracker biscuits.

"Ooh! Jake thought—this looks good", drooling at the mouth at the sight of the food and wolfed it down.

Meanwhile Nigel removed his filthy dressing gown and pyjamas, because both were soiled with Jake's dirt, and put clean night attire on before sitting on the settee with Jake sitting beside him with his head resting against Nigel, each trying to communicate with the other. They were devoted to one another and shared a deep bond and were absolutely elated in a quiet manner to be together again.

Five weeks after his return home tragedy struck. Nigel had completed his morning ablutions and had come downstairs to let Jake run into the back garden to relieve himself.

"Morning boy—wake up and come along outside", called Nigel. But Jake just sat on his haunches in his basket. No amount of persuasion could get Jake moving without help. "We'll have breakfast first then". Again there was no usual response from Jake who was wriggling and whining. Nigel physically lifted Jake out of his basket and quickly discovered that Jake had completely lost all movement in his hindquarters. In wheelbarrow fashion Nigel helped Jake into the garden to do what he had to do and brought him back into the house the same way. Nigel had to help him eat and drink from his food and drinking bowls. Nigel was astonished and profoundly worried by the situation that his healthy fun-loving animal was now only partially mobile.

Nigel advised his boss by telephone that he would not be at work as it was imperative to take his dear old Jake to the veterinary hospital. Fortunately his boss had a pet too so was very understanding and told Nigel to take as much time as needed. It was a struggle for Nigel to lift Jake in and out of the car. At the hospital Jake was thoroughly examined and tests made by the vet, Ron Taylor, a very experienced vet, to find out what was the cause of Jake's sudden loss of movement. Ron was not able to firmly identify the cause of Jake's problem and would have to wait for the test results to establish the cause of loss of movement. Meanwhile he prescribed some pain relief tablets because it was obvious that Jake was in some distress. Ron tried to soothe Jake. He said, *"If you want to get well soon—you've got to take a tablet of two boy—you've got to take a tablet or two"*—(not—*pick a pocket or two* from the musical of Charles Dickens **Oliver**).

As arranged, three days later, with no visible improvement in Jake's condition, Nigel took Jake back to the hospital. Ron Taylor was not able to enlighten Nigel at this point in time but thought that Jake's was suffering from paralysis with little hope of recovery. Ron, very bluntly, gave Nigel two options. Either tolerate and cope with Jake's affliction or have him put to sleep. Nigel rejected the latter option and explained the recent incident of Jake going missing and finding his way back home. This demonstrated to the vet, beyond doubt, the bond and devotion that held Nigel and Jake together. It was pure conjecture but the vet believed Jake's affliction had probably been caused by the stress and anxiety Jake underwent in finding his way home from Walton-on-the-Naze. The vet advised Nigel that it would help if Jake could have some therapy. For example, putting him into a bath or tub with warm water and massaging his rear legs. The Vet thought this would be helpful but quite costly. Nigel was not concerned about the cost or time taken with the therapy because he was determined that in Jake's time of need he, Nigel, would not let him down. But, before this could be done Ron Taylor suggested that Jake should spend some time in the veterinary hospital so that the vets could observe him more fully and perhaps run more tests. During this time Nigel would not be allowed to visit Jake as it was considered this to be very unsettling for the hound.

Nigel returned with Jake to the hospital a few days later and was told that it was not certain at the time of his admission how long Jake would need to remain there. Nigel returned home alone, depressed and lonely, his mind on how poor Jake would feel being parted from him again. The hardest part to swallow was being told that he could not visit Jake in hospital but he telephoned the hospital daily to find out if any progress had been made.

Some weeks later Nigel received a 'phone call to say he could collect and take Jake home but that Jake would need to be taken for 'swimming lessons'. In other words therapy sessions to try and get some movement into Jake's rear limbs. Master and his pal were delighted to be re-united again.

Months passed and Nigel had to physically hump and move Jake around—in a wheelbarrow fashion—until eventually the hospital suggested that Nigel might wish to try Jake in a harness on a trolley type frame so that Nigel could take Jake for short walks until Jake became used to being more mobile. The straps of the trolley would take some time for Jake to adapt to because, although his front paws touched the ground, his hindquarters were raised so that his back paws did not drag on the ground.

The trolley, a light-weight contraption, with two large wheels—about eighteen inches in diameter—and fitted to a light alloy frame with nylon straps that were buckled underneath Jake's body, enabled Jake to move around unassisted. Nigel had overall control as he attached Jakes lead to the harness.

Nigel found that with the use of the trolley Jake was able to walk a little farther each day. It was also a blessing because the strain of physically lifting Jake in and out of the house had been quite a strain on Nigel.

Nigel sat on his settee one late evening, after their walk, with Jake resting his head on Nigel's lap, whilst Nigel was gently stroking Jake's head and thinking how extremely grateful he was for the company of a not so dumb animal. There was an air of peace all around. Nigel glanced up to the ceiling and he heard a 'still small voice quietly say to him':

*I am the night the day, the blessing and the way, and
Whatever you do for the least of my creatures—is that you do unto me.*

* * *

Although, sadly, Jake is still partially paralysed master and his pal are able to go '*walkies*' around the lanes and Jake's favourite field. Apart from his affliction he is now quite a healthy dog and Nigel and Jake live quite happily together. Below is a photograph, taken in the author's garden, of Jake wearing his harness.

THE END

Epilogue from Nigel

I wish firstly to take this opportunity to thank Cyril for making Jake and myself the subjects of this story. It gives me great pride that he should feel that we are worthy of such an accolade.

With regards to the situation with Jake and myself, as Cyril has stated, the story is fictitious, but the basis of the story, Jakes disability, is very real.

The way Jake has dealt with his paralysis has had a massive impression on me, and my outlook on life. The very sudden onset happened when he was just three years old and still a puppy really. Once I had been assured by the specialist consultant, that he was in no pain and that I could give him as much time as I needed, to see if he could recover, I made it my mission in life to help him have as much of a life as possible, by any sacrifice to my own lifestyle if necessary. I felt he was worth that and that I owed him that much.

Jake had helped me come through the worst year of my life, through ill health, and had given me the reason to keep going. Now was payback time. The doctors told me that there was nothing they could do for my condition and that I would have to learn to live with it. So when I heard the same prognosis about Jake, I just knew we would have to prove that we could get through it again, but this time in reversed roles.

Jake had physiotherapy administered by myself three time a day, hydrotherapy sessions at our local vets three times a week and acupuncture, as well as some natural remedies that we tried, all to try and help the strength and feelings return to his rear legs and tail. And what a patient he was! He has such a good temperament, that he allowed anything to be done to him without a blink of his eye. Over several months of all this treatment, some very good improvements did come. He can wag his tail as before, and can use his right rear leg almost as normal now, but his left rear leg remains only about fifty percent recovered. He can also stand for short periods of time to eat his dinner.

After seven months of this, it was apparent that his improvement had reached a plateau situation and no longer appeared to be making any further improvement. I had already sourced a doggie wheelchair through the Internet, but had refrained from using it, as per instruction of the specialist. He now advised me to start using it.

I was very apprehensive about this at first, as I worried about how other people would feel about it. I had seen small dogs in wheelchairs on TV, but wasn't sure how I felt about them. However, I decided I just wanted to give Jake a bit of a life, even if it was only for a couple of years, as he was so young still. So I took the plunge, and not only did it transform our lives and give Jake his life back, but to my delight the vast majority of people we met on our walks were very curious and understanding. Once I had told them about the whole situation, and that there may still be some improvement as time went on, and most importantly, that he was in no pain, they all gave me great support, including Cyril and his wife Patricia.

I would strongly encourage anyone who sees a dog in a wheelchair, to approach the owner and ask about the predicament. I usually find that the people who take the moral high ground are the people who don't ask the questions and therefore do not get the answers. I have always said to everyone, that as long as Jake is free from pain and appears happy with his life, then I would give him as long as I can, hopefully his full natural term of life. And he is happy in his life. I've had dogs all my life and have never known one who seems so content. He is a great inspiration. He still enjoys his walkies, or wheelies as we now call it. He loves nothing better than running around the field with the other dogs, and is still notorious amongst the cat population of the area, as he still gives chase when he catches me unawares.

But looking to the future, there is hope on the horizon. Research trials are being held regarding a stem cell operation, aiming to help paralysed people walk again. Trials were carried out on rats and are now being carried out on dogs. These dogs are all in a similar state as Jake and have been volunteered by their owners to try to help their situation. Jake has his name down, but is currently eliminated from the trials by his size. They are only carrying it out on dogs under 20 kg at this stage, so not much chance for a Belgian Shepherd! But they have assured me that if the trial is successful, that it will be put out as treatment across the board. So fingers and everything else crossed, it will be successful, not only for dogs but ultimately for humans, and Jake will get the boost that he needs to get fully mobile again.

So, to anyone who finds they are in a similar predicament, I would encourage you take inspiration from Jake and to investigate the feasibility of using a wheelchair, providing the animal is in no pain and is in a happy, comfortable state. You will need patience, dedication and to be able to devote time and assistance. But if you are like me, you will find it a very rewarding experience. It has vastly increased the already incredible bond that existed between Jake and myself.

I would again like to thank Cyril and Patricia. I would also like to thank my dad Dave and his partner Sylvi for their help and support, especially for taking Jake in to allow me much-needed holiday breaks. Also I must give a massive thank you to Shelly and Lorraine at my local vets, who along with Nikki previously and others who have stepped in to assist, have shown great dedication and perseverance in helping Jake.

Also thanks to all the people who ask about, encourage and support me when out and about with Jake, and thank you for reading this story.

My last thanks must go to Jake for being such an amazing friend. When I first went to see Jake when looking for a puppy, he was in a pen with three other three-month old puppies, wriggled through a small gap in the gate, ran passed three other people, including my dad and Sylvi, and jumped straight up into my arms. He "picked" me not the other way around! Either that or he knows a mug when he sees one.

And finally to any doubters, I would say just one thing; **if you could only see what I see you would understand.**

Thank you

Nigel

Trade Secret

....

Dedicated to John Wells and his good humoured, fun loving, family.

The Secret family consisted of father, mother, five sons, their wives and partners and their offspring. The whole family shared buildings converted into pleasant living accommodation on farmland. The five sons' names were John, Jim, Joe, Jesse and Jack. John being the eldest and Jack the youngest of the brothers. Their father Jim was always subordinate to John in business affairs whereas the sons' mother Mary had complete control over domestic matters.

The complication of all the boys' names, including that of the father, beginning with 'J' caused constant friction amongst them when the mail was delivered. They had to open each piece of mail to ascertain for which 'Mr. J. Secret' the mail was intended and when an item of mail was marked 'confidential' this became an even greater problem and on several occasions caused father Jim and mother Mary to contemplate having the boys re-christened. However, Mary was very reluctant to do so because she had a weird vision of the christening entailing the help of perhaps two strong fellows, maybe bouncers, to lift each of her burly sons into the christening font. They had even considered fresh names for the boys, such as, Julius, Horatio, Rudyard, Charlie and Henry. Jim was unable to convince Mary, or to assure her, that re-christening would not need the help of bouncers and that the vicar would only douse their heads with either a mug full or saucepan full of holy water.

"Won't the lads catch a death of cold?" enquired Mary.

"No! Of course not, they are healthy fellows, except Jack with his recurring tennis elbow", replied Jim reassuringly. The family were not churchgoers so they never did follow through with their intention, although the idea was not entirely kicked into the long grass. On one occasion the boys argued over an important letter. Jim, the boys' father, decided to intervene by proffering some advice, "remember lads, Charlie Chan says to his number one son— *"Confucius, he say—***mind like parachute, only works when open***"* (i.e. Charlie Chan from the Charlie Chan film series). Jim was frequently reciting the adages of Confucius. Jesse felt that his dad must have a hot line to Confucius and often expressed his feelings on the subject.

Jim, the father, and his five sons worked as a small company sharing all the proceeds from their work. John, the eldest, acted as chief executive and provided quotes and estimates and made the arrangements for each of their assignments. He also collected the payments from their customers whereas Jack, the youngest brother, who was often misunderstood as he likewise often misunderstood those he dealt with and really only helped his brothers, because he was receiving incapacity benefit from the state for his tennis elbow, but was very skilled with the chain saw. John was a very skilful tree surgeon but with the company of his dad and brothers they undertook various jobs like garden landscaping, trimming of shrubs, lopping or removal of trees, catching mice or rats that were infesting homes and gardens, laying concrete slabs or laying driveways for the householders. No job was too big, too small, or two complicated for them. They would do any and every job and built up a reputation for being reliable, quick, thorough and clean workers. They were hardly ever short of work.

There was one recent assignment that posed a problem that John resolved. It was a job requested by Mr and Mrs Puddifoot for John to trim the hedge surrounding the front garden belonging to the couple. John negotiated with the couple and arranged to carry out the job. The hedge and fence was only broken by the front gate and a cherry tree growing next to the road pavement side of the fence, which caused the fencer who erected the fence to leave a break in the fence to accommodate the cherry tree because Thelma Puddifoot did not want the tree removed as it was beautiful when in bloom in springtime. Thelma was a fairly elderly woman who had complete control over all their affairs because her husband was wheelchair bound with acute arthritis.

The Secret brothers, on the same day as their assignment with Mrs Puddifoot, also undertook the preparation of a driveway to the frontage of a house some three hundred yards down the same road as that of Mrs Puddifoot. It was not a main road but nevertheless a fairly busy one and the other customer wanted to be able to park a car off the road and on the driveway. John, who was also skilful with the hedge trimmers, with the help of his dad, trimmed Mrs Puddifoot's hedge and when he had finished asked jack to clear up all the clippings and place them on a large canvas sheet that they had brought with them. He said to Jack, "I want you to leave this area scrupulously clean". This instruction caused Jim, their dad, to quote another adage,

"Confucius, he say, '*he who has broom will be screw-u-pusshly clean*'".

"Dad, you can't say things like that".

"Son, Confucius, he would say, '*man with mind like cesspool will misinterpret things men say and how they say it!*' Confucius was a very clever, ancient, Chinese philosopher son", dad added.

"When you have done that Jack would you deal with that cherry tree and then see Mrs Puddifoot as she has an erection in her back garden, supporting a honeysuckle shrub, which is leaning over. Be a good lad and straighten it up for her—you may need to hammer in the ground fixings—okay?"

"Okay John, I'll do that", replied Jack.

"Dad and I will be going along to help Jesse, Jim and Joe and we won't be long", advised John, before leaving Jack on his own.

Jack, as usual, had misunderstood the instruction with regard to the cherry tree. When dad and his brothers returned they were happy with the clean up but astounded that the cherry tree had been completely removed down to ground level. Jack had lopped off all the branches. All that was left was a six feet length of straight trunk on the pavement. John was very angry because he would have to do some unnecessary explaining to Mrs Puddifoot, whereas dad Jim saw the amusing side of the situation and quoted another adage, "Confucius, he say, **he who has chelly tree will always be velly fluity**".

"Shut up dad, this is not funny admonished John".

The father noticed a rather nasty swelling on Jack's wrist. "What have you done there boy?" he enquired.

"Oh, I clonked my wrist when I was dealing with that erection in the back garden".

"You had better take the truck and go to that surgery down the road and have it wrapped up", advised his dad and the others all agreed.

Meanwhile John had the embarrassing task of explaining to Mrs Puddifoot the awful mistake Jack had made. Jack had not understood the instructions he was given and had removed the cherry tree by mistake. Mrs Puddifoot, in her annoyance, was adamant that something must be done to rectify the situation and rejected John's suggestion that he could install a nine-foot long concrete clothes post in place of the tree against which Mrs P. could plant a shrub of the climbing variety to grow up the post.

Before Jack drove off to go to the surgery he was asked to call in at the nearby supermarket and pick up a few bits and pieces their mother had asked the lads to get. A couple of the items would be needed for their evening meal.

Jack entered the surgery and was surprised to find only two people waiting to be seen by a doctor. He reported to 'reception' and the receptionist asked, "Can I help you?"

"Yea, can I see a doctor?" replied Jack.

"Yes, what's your name?"

"My name is Secret".

"Listen, don't wind me up. I remember you came here over three weeks ago and told me your name was Mud and when I asked you whether it was spelled with a single 'D' or double 'D' you told me that the 'D' was silent as in biscuits—then you promptly disappeared. Now, I'll ask you again, what is your name—your proper name?"

"My proper name is Secret—Jack Secret—and my address is—and he quoted his address".

"Now we're getting somewhere. Briefly, what is your complaint?" asked the receptionist.

"I have a swollen, painful wrist", replied Jack.

"What has caused that", queried the receptionist.

"Well I was dealing with an erection and I hurt my wrist in the process", Jack replied.

"Is the erection still there".

"Oh yea, very much so, but it's quite straight now", Jack answered.

The receptionist then asked Jack to take a seat and told him that he would be called as soon as the two patients had been attended to. When Jack entered the consulting room of Doctor Theodora Willy he was startled to see sitting on her table, in addition to her computer, an array of hypodermic needles, a kidney dish, a blood pressure test meter and some other medical instruments. The sight of these frightened the life out of him and his fear caused him to run out of the surgery as fast as he could.

"I'm not having her poking around my arm with all that stuff—s—it! I'll go to the supermarket", now thought Jack. His father had given him a short list of his mother's requirements and told him to go to the supermarket near the surgery where he would find all the items. However, there were five items he could not find on the shelves so he sought the help of a shop assistant who was busy stacking the empty shelves with goods.

"Excuse me, do you have any beansprouts?"

"Yes, we have runner beans and brussel sprouts—would that be okay?"

"No, not really, replied Jack and went on to ask,

"Do you have any tins of broad beans?"

"I am sorry, broad beans are out of season".

"What about packets of self-raising flour?"

"No, I'm afraid flour is out of stock", the assistant replied.

Jack was disappointed because without flour they would not be able to have a Yorkshire pudding that evening with their meat and Jack loved Yorkshire pudding. He searched around the shelves and found a nicely illustrated packet of Yorkshire pudding mix. There were two other items he could not get. "This will have to do", he thought and wheeled his trolley to the cash till to pay for his shopping, loaded the van and drove off to pick up his dad and brothers.

When he arrived back to the others his dad asked him,

"How did you get on at the surgery?"

"Oh, all right", and lying through his teeth explained, "the doctor advised me to use some embrocation on my wrist". Jack was too ashamed to tell the truth.

It was then that Jim came up with an idea. "Listen Jack, you are going to France on a week's holiday next week so, while you are there, make your way to Lourdes for a miracle cure. A couple of prayers and you'll be completely cured".

"Did you say Lords? I'm not interested in cricket".

"No, I said Lourdes".

"No way", responded Jack. "The cure will probably cure my tennis elbow as well and then I'll lose my incapacity benefit".

"Sorry, I hadn't thought of that", said Jim. "Anyway, what about the shopping, did you get it all?" asked his dad.

"No, there were five items I couldn't get even though I asked the shop assistant to help".

"What did she say?"

"She said they had plenty of runner beans and brussel sprouts instead of bean sprouts and when I asked about tinned broad beans she said they were out of season.

"Out of season—what, tins of broad beans!" retorted Jim.

"I couldn't get flour either, it was out of stock but I did get a packet of Yorkshire pudding mix".

Jack's dad rummaged through the shopping bags and pulled out the packet of mix. He promptly started reading the instructions on the packet. He then called to the lads for their attention.

"Hey, you lot, listen to this and I am reading it off the back of this packet. The cooking instructions say that the contents of the packet should be emptied into a suitable bowl. Then add a half a teaspoon of baking powder, one egg, two tablespoonfuls of milk, four tablespoons of water, season to taste then mix until a running mixture results. Then place in a greased dish and bake in the oven for half an hour at gas mark eight. Well, what do you know?"

"What's wrong with that?" asked Joe.

"I'll tell you. If you need to add all that stuff then the packet must only contain plain flour and it's priced at £1.95p. We could buy a ready-to-eat plum pudding for that price", retorted Jim exasperatingly. "It's a real take-on!" he added.

"Did you get the cans of Bass beer and the bag of sugar?"

"I went to the drinks section and I couldn't see any Bass. When I asked the bloke there he said that they didn't do fish in bottles, and when I asked about a 2lb bag of sugar the woman said that they only sold sugar in KILOMETRES. I have no idea what a kilometre is".*

Jack's father was speechless but he did advise Jack to spray his wrist with WD40 (a general purpose lubricant) from the can stored in the cab of their truck.

On another occasion, a few days earlier, whilst exchanging banter with three workmen who were replacing perfectly suitable and in good condition bus stop posts with a new type. John was able to 'acquire' one of the old bus stop posts to take to his farmyard. He had no idea how he would put it to use. The new posts were fitted with a touch type panel and powered by a solar panel mounted at the top of the post. When touched the panel was activated for passengers to select the information they required, such as bus arrival and departure times, etc., in other words a speaking timetable. The workmen advised John, rather cynically, that it was designed not only to save electricity but would save the bus company money. When, during a cloudy day and after darkness, the solar panel lay dormant, people waiting for a bus would not be able to consult a printed display timetable.

The company had withdrawn printed timetable leaflets and booklets so 'would be' passengers would not be able to complain about non-arrival, or late arrival, of buses. This would allow the company to withdraw or reduce certain services thereby saving money to enhance their profits—all in the noble art of customer service. Passengers would not have any grounds for complaint. John accepted the cynicisms.

---

* *The banter between Jack and the shop assistant and Jack and his dad is courtesy of the 'letters' page of the Daily Telegraph.*

When the lads arrived back at their farmyard Joe suddenly burst forth, "I have an idea. Why don't we use the old bus stop post to fill the gap left in the fence at Mrs Puddifoot's. He suggested that the post—which he cynically claimed to be organic—could be installed between the ground level cherry tree stump and the pavement edge by using some ready-mix, quick setting, concrete to secure it. After giving it some thought Jim, the father, and the brothers agreed that it was a brilliant suggestion especially as the bus stop post was in a good clean condition and still displaying a timetable. They all agreed that it would not be an eye sore and agreed the job should be carried out the following day.

The installation was completed the following morning, as agreed, before they proceeded to another more taxing job.

That evening John received a rather truculent 'phone call from Mrs Puddifoot who complained, rather bitterly, that she wanted the bus stop removed because she approached, on several occasions, people waiting at the bus stop. Mrs Puddifoot had to explain to them that it was not in use and the nearest bus route was extant. John apologized profusely and suggested that they would have to think of an alternative measure. John, who was a tree surgeon, had a running contract with the local hospital to work in the hospital grounds, lopping and removing any unwanted or obstructive branches from the perimeter trees and those adjacent to the hospital thoroughfares. This work he carried out every Thursday and when Mrs Puddifoot suggested he remove the objectionable bus stop from her fence perimeter the next day—Thursday—John advised "I'm sorry we cannot do it tomorrow because I carry out 'surgery' at the hospital and the others are on another job. We will remove it on Friday". They would have to think of another solution to satisfy Mrs Puddifoot.

When Mrs Puddifoot replaced the telephone receiver on its cradle her husband asked, "What was the result?"

Mr. Secret (John) says he cannot remove the bus stop tomorrow as I suggested because he does surgery at the hospital. He'll do it on Friday".

"Surgery! What sort of surgery?" he asked with a note of surprise in his voice.

"I don't know—perhaps hip replacements, kidney transplants, removal of an appendix, removal of gall stones, that sort of thing".

"Well, well, he must be a clever dexterous fellow, especially when he chops down trees and trims shrubs the rest of the week".

"I suppose he must be very clever doing all that sort of work", she agreed.

When the boys had returned to the farm, all in a contemplative mood, an idea struck Jesse as a solution to Mrs Puddifoot's gap. He expressed his idea enthusiastically. "You know the cherry tree trunk that has been lying in the yard—why don't we take it back and fix it to the stump?"

The father pointed out that it would be a very tricky job that would need some kind of additional support. Moreover, it would be an eye sore.

"Not really", Jesse said. "If we drill three or four holes in the base of the trunk with matching holes in the stump, we could drive steel rods into the base and, with the addition of a tube of 'no more nails' adhesive, fix it back by pushing the trunk on to the rods in the base".

As soon as Jesse's dad heard the word 'rods' mentioned he piped up—"Confucius, he say, '*he who has fishing rod will have whale of a time*'".

"Shut up dad—try and be serious for Gawd's sake", admonished Jesse.

John wasn't completely convinced that the idea would work but was prepared to give it a try, subject to the approval of Mrs Puddifoot, especially when Jim suggested that Jack—a dab hand with the chainsaw—could carve a profile of a man with a head, eyes, ears, nose and mouth to make the trunk represent a figure—a kind of totem pole. Joe suggested sticking and stapling some straw on top of the proposed head to represent hair, but not too much otherwise the totem, now named **Wally**, would need a haircut.

Mrs Puddifoot was not entirely impressed with the novelty of a totem pole so near to her fence but she had no alternative in accepting it as a very temporary measure and so it was arranged for Jim, John and the gang to go ahead.

The boys had brought with them the bare tree trunk, short steel rods, adhesive, some batons and slats and ironmongery. Firstly they filled in the fence gap by nailing batons and slats to the existing fence. Some two hours later, after a lot of palaver, errors and pushing and pulling, the trunk was erected on to the stump. Jack immediately collected an old milk crate from the back of the truck, to stand on, to give him height so that he could carve the head and its features. He even carved five vertically spaced indentations in Wally's chest to represent buttons. Jessy then stepped on to the milk crate and fixed some straw on top of Wally's head with adhesive and staples. Wally looked quite a smart guy by the time they had finished the job.

Several days later, during which time, passers by and others who had heard about what had happened were curious to see the finished product. This resulted in one of the Bucks Herald, (the local newspaper), journalists, a photographer and a reporter joining the crowd that gathered to view, photograph and report on 'Wally the totem pole'. The reporter approached Mrs Puddifoot to enquire about the history of the totem pole. Mrs Puddifoot explained how this all arose and that the project had been executed by the male members of the 'Secret' family. The reporter thought it would be an interesting topic for inclusion, together with the photographs, in the next edition of the newspaper.

"Hey! Look lads, our name and our totem pole—Wally—is in the paper this week", shouted Jim excitedly clutching the newspaper. Jim (senior) and brothers dropped what they were doing to peer at the three published pictures of Wally and hastily read the report that was very complimentary of their imagination and skill in overcoming and making good their error.

"You know what", said Joe excitedly. This is good publicity for us and this should step up our business prospects. We could prosper and grow and then expand to become a big international company with offices in London, Paris, Rome and Berlin. John could be the chief executive and the rest of us executives of the overseas branches—except Jack. He will not want to loose his incapacity benefit but he could be our mascot".

Unfortunately his dad and brothers were not enthusiastic, or as optimistic, as Joe but they did not entirely reject Joe's imaginative suggestion.

"By what name would the company trade under?" asked Jim (senior).

"Well, what about something like, a, *International Trade Secrets*, or *Secret Company*,—how about that?"

"That's a bit daft", retorted John. "We don't trade secretly and we don't harbour secrets and we don't want to be an international company. But I must say, with all this publicity our company can grow and diversify—or will it?"

YOU MAY THINK THAT THIS IS THE END—WELL IT IS!

THE END

The Happy One

1809-1847

Felix Mendelssohn-Bartholdy
Brief Biography

In memory of the late Robert Heath who was a happy person

There are not many who are unfamiliar with the much loved song, *Oh, for the wings of a Dove*. At Christmas time, however people assemble to sing or play carols, an old favourite that is featured at almost every event is *Hark the herald angels sing*. It is almost safe to say that on every day of the year, somewhere in the world, the beautiful strains of the *Wedding March* will be heard echoing through churches to celebrate the joyful occasion. This music is performed with such regularity that it is taken for granted without a shred of thought being paid to the person who composed it. Who was this person? He was none other than 'the most brilliant musician who ever lived' (a description given to him by Robert Schumann). He remains 'unequalled' even to this day. Doubtless two bold statements but let us examine the man, his music and his contribution to the art. **Felix—the happy one**, passed through life on the wings of a song.

Felix Mendelssohn was born on the third of February 1809, in Hamburg, Germany. His father was a wealthy banker and his mother a well-educated, cultured woman. He was the second of four children and Felix was always devoted to his family, although he held a special affection for his elder sister Fanny that was to last throughout his lifetime. They were a Jewish family who later embraced the Christian faith and adopted the Christian name of Bartholdy, Felix's uncle's name. The family belonged to the 'bourgeoisie set' in Hamburg and the children were brought up under very strict codes of conduct and discipline. From a very early age Felix was made to rise at 5 o'clock every morning to commence his studies. Music was only one of the many subjects in which he received a thorough education.

Later in life, nothing irritated Felix more than to have to discuss music when in company. Whereas, being a qualified philosopher, a fluent linguist in Greek, Latin and English, qualified in the art of literature, both German and English and no mean artist in water-colours, these subjects he longed to discuss when in the right company. Mendelssohn is one of only three child prodigies to be found in the world of music, the others being of course Mozart and Schubert.

We shall later see the paradox one finds between the life of Mozart and that of Mendelssohn.

Mozart was from a modest background whose father, recognising the boy's genius, did everything possible to bring his son's talent to the attention of the musical world. This was not so with Mendelssohn. His parents would have preferred him to follow a career in either banking or law and, after many family disagreements, it was settled that the boy should follow a musical career.

When the family moved to Berlin Mendelssohn was nine years old. Adjoining their large house in the city was a beautiful garden that Felix loved. It was his fascination of the garden that set in train his wish to put Shakespeare's *Midsummer Night's Dream* to music. He was well versed in all of Shakespeare's plays. It was not until he was sixteen that his wish came to fruition when he gave the world the overture to the *"Dream"*. As a twelve year old he said to his family, "Today or tomorrow I shall dream the 'Midsummer's Dream'". The overture received international acclaim almost immediately.

Paradoxically Mozart did not receive international fame until well after his death. The *Octet in E flat major* soon followed the success of the overture and in this respect Mendelssohn eclipsed Mozart.

From the age of four Felix and his sister Fanny would give piano concerts on Sunday afternoons at the family home when friends and relatives would be invited. The musicales much later included young brother Paul playing the cello and sister Rebecca who would sing. These family sessions over a period of time attracted more and more strangers into the audience and Felix's reputation as a pianist and, later, organist grew throughout Europe to the extent that by the time he had reached his early twenties he was regarded as being Europe's finest and most brilliant pianist and organist. He was accomplished and could play many other orchestral instruments.

Although Mozart was highly regarded as a pianist he never achieved such international fame in his youth, nor was he so fortunate as to have a wealthy family to assist and support him in his early years.

Mendelssohn was constantly conscious of his good fortune and it had a definite effect on his approach to life and his music. He was always cautious and conservative, coupled with this was the lifelong stigma of being born a Jew. This caused him to write music that would please his audience and desisted from being too radical. However, many ideas of his that came to fruition in his music, when compared with several of his predecessors and contemporaries, were undoubtedly worthy of attention. He was endowed with 'perfect pitch' and a unique sense of recall. It is said that his sense of recall was so acute that in his early twenties he was able to play every note of the nine Beethoven symphonies, on the piano, by memory, and often did this to the delight of uninvited audiences. (Charles Halle grossly exaggerated when he claimed Mendelssohn could recall every note ever written).

In his early twenties Mendelssohn began his travels through Europe and the British Isles. He visited all the major European capitals giving concerts. His later visits were for a different purpose. He was taken to meet the great literary master and poet Goethe who was so impressed with him that he made Mendelssohn play the piano to him for several hours. Mendelssohn dedicated the *Spring Song* to Goethe. Being a man of sunny and friendly disposition he made many, many, friends throughout Europe. Included amongst these were Queen Victoria, Prince Albert, King of Prussia, Sir Walter Scott, Sir Robert Peel, and Charles Halle. He regarded them all as personal friends. He was also a personal friend of Schumann, Chopin, Berlioz and Wagner. Wagner was somewhat critical of Mendelssohn yet used some of Mendelssohn ideas in his own compositions. It was Wagner who criticised him for being careful and over cautious. Yet Queen Victoria thought his music was somewhat radical. Her Majesty preferred uncomplicated music. Mendelssohn made several visits to Windsor Castle on the invitation of the Queen and on one occasion, after he had already played the piano to the Queen for several hours, and by that time felt quite exhausted, he stopped.

Queen Victoria was an avid listener and implored him to play on. "Play on Mr. Mendelssohn, do play on". He continued to play until he nearly collapsed at the keyboard. This incident caused The Queen to invite him to Balmoral Castle for a holiday and he used this period to tour Scotland and loved it.

Because of his numerous visits to Britain he was regarded the second Handel. He was invited to settle in Britain, but being German and a great family man his longing to be at home was too great. His close family ties and constant hard work kept him so busy that there could never be any scandal attached to him. He loved his home and family, enjoyed the company of friends and relatives and delighted in constant hard work. He also had a passionate love of nature and his music is regarded as the most descriptive in the repertoire.

Mr. Mendelssohn also had a passionate love for the music of Bach, Beethoven, Mozart, Haydn and Schubert. At seventeen years old he discovered Bach's *St. Matthew Passion* buried in the vaults of a Berlin museum. He immediately studied it and set about assembling an orchestra, a chorus of four hundred, and solo, singers to resurrect and perform the work. He re-orchestrated much of it so it would be more acceptable as a concert work. This was no mean achievement for somebody of his age in those days and the eventual performance in Liepzig was a resounding success. It received further success in Berlin. This event led him to delve further into the archives where he found several Beethoven works, notably the Seventh and Pastoral symphonies, also many of Mozart's works. Had it not been for Mr. Mendelssohn many of the much-loved works of these three great composers, and others, would have been lost to posterity. He spent most of his life returning to the European capitals giving performances of the great masters at his own expense, and often at the expense of his own music. He strove unceasingly to promote their music and some regarded him as the 'St. Paul' of music—(ironically one of Mr. Mendelssohn's well-known oratorios is *St. Paul.*

In Mr. Mendelssohn's day it was accepted practice that a symphony, for example, would never be played in its entirely. The movements were interspersed with other, different, short pieces. He changed this and insisted on the full work being performed. This content and practice is carried on to this day. He also increased the size of the orchestra from around twenty musicians to its present day size. He wanted the world to hear the fullness and beauty of Bach's, Mozart's, Schumann's, Chopin's and Schubert's music. He was the first conductor to use a baton and the first to have the audience face the orchestra. Since he financed many of the concerts him self they were open to all who were keen to listen. He tried tirelessly to bring music to the ordinary people. Musical appreciation was no longer the preserve of the aristocracy—thanks to Mendelssohn. Had he not composed one piece of music himself, he would nevertheless be famous for his work of promoting the enjoyment of the music of the 'great composers' for the ordinary people.

Mr. Mendelssohn was described by the eminent conductor Hans von Bulow as a 'romantic classicist' but, as previously mentioned, he was always regarded by his contemporaries and music critics as being too conservative and cautious—(he had nothing new to say in his music—he had no fresh ideas—his music is dull and lacks imagination but of course pleasant to listen to). These criticisms are not justified. If we take into account his strict, disciplined, upbringing—made to rise at 5 a.m. each morning when a child, a practice he continued to the end of his life; his very close family relationship—his mother being the main influence—the fact that he was a wealthy Christian Jew amongst nationalistic protestant Germans. In addition, Hitler had all his music destroyed in 1937. All this must have had a tremendous bearing on his sensitivity, attitude and approach to life. As a conductor he demanded total dedication and discipline from the orchestra. The musicians regarded him as a tyrant, but in his music he strove to please his audiences—hence the adage *as sweet as a Mendelssohn tune*. He was not a prolific composer except when he was a youth but, tragically, most of his youthful works were destroyed by the Nazi regime. Unlike Mozart he received international acclaim when still a youth with the *Octet in E flat* and the *Midsummer's Night Dream* overture. By this time he had also composed nine operas and a host of piano and organ works, not now in the repertoire.

Tchaikovsky was so impressed with the '*Dream*' overture that he said it was this music that opened the way to his own fairytale ideas, but modestly conceded that he could not easily reproduce the light tripping elfin effect of Mendelssohn's music. Both Rimsky-Korsakov and Wagner were impressed by Mr. Mendelssohn's ideas but Wagner was too proud to publicly admit it. Meyerbeer, the French composer, although a critic of the over-cautious Mendelssohn, recognized that he had opened up a field of descriptive music. Wagner secretly described Mendelssohn as a 'landscape painter in music' and Berlioz, Mr. Mendelssohn's friend, whilst praiseworthy of his idea of enlarging the orchestra to its present day size, criticised him for not going further in its enlargement. All were extremely praiseworthy of Mendelssohn's concert programming that continues to be used to the present day. "A great work must be played in its entirety or not at all" was his maxim.

Although brilliant at orchestrating and being a composer of delightfully descriptive music, the twelve string symphonies are unusual in their construction being confined mainly to string instruments. They are in the classical Italian style of three movements. He composed these between the age of twelve and fourteen years of age. Of Mendelssohn's other five symphonies for full orchestra four are in the forefront of the great symphonies in the repertoire. Mendelssohn's second symphony in B flat, Opus 52 *Lobgesang—Hymn of Praise* follows sonata form generally until it reaches the last movement, (a choral movement), containing a series of canticles derived from the Book of Psalms, the most well known and beloved piece being *Now thank we all our God with hands and soul and voice*s, a popular hymn even today. He was not a practising Christian but believed that the supreme act of worship lay in one's consideration for others. He endeavoured to practice this belief often at great expense to himself—an unselfish individual always willing to offer help to those less fortunate than himself. Mendelssohn's second symphony was commissioned to celebrate the four centuries anniversary of the printing press and the solemn unveiling of the memorial to Gutenburg at Leipzig.

Symphony number three in A minor—Opus 56—*The Scottish* resulted from inspiration he received when on a tour of Scotland and as a guest of the Queen at Balmoral where he was fascinated with the story of Mary Queen of Scots. He was so enraptured by the Scottish scene, its atmosphere, its people, its ruggedness that in a letter to his sister Fanny said, "I feel I have found the beginnings of my Scottish Symphony". Apart from being a supremely descriptive work, Mr. Mendelssohn broke new ground in symphonic construction by employing the Scottish folk dance pentatonic scale (that is the omission of the fourth and seventh notes of the diatonic scale) to a the slow third movement; a feature never before or since attempted in classical work. It took him thirteen years to complete and he constantly revised it in an attempt to achieve perfection. He was never completely satisfied with it and refused to accept at any stage that the version was final. He dedicated the Symphony to Queen Victoria and when it was eventually performed no less than twenty-nine consecutive performances, to a packed concert hall, were given at the Gewendhaus, Leipzig's famous theatre. No other symphony or other work has had such a resounding success. It is ironic that it was a German Jew who composed the Scottish Symphony and a subtle reminder of this can be heard in the coda of the last movement when we hear a fanfare by the French horns, reminiscent of the German woodland scene. The storm scene of the first movement pointed the way for Wagner's *Flying Dutchman* and Rimsky-Korsakov's *Sea and Sinbad's Ship* in *Scheherazade*.

Again, it took a German Jew to compose the *Italian Symphony—Symphony number one in A Major, Opus 90*, and Mr. Mendelssohn received inspiration for this when he was on a long tour of Italy. It is a vibrant symphony that truly reflects the mood of the Italian people and the Italian scene but which had its first performance in London. He did however become quite disappointed with their behaviour and 'devil may care' attitude and could not reconcile this with his belief of Italy being the cradle of art, music and culture. He longed to return home to his family and this longing is again present in the third movement, a pastoral movement—not Italian but German, where the haunting horn fanfare portrays the mood and again the German woodland scene. The fourth movement represents an Italian Fiesta—compare the triplets to that of *The Festival of Baghdad* in *Scheherazade*.

Mendelssohn's fifth symphony in D Minor, Opus 107, owes its existence to a historical occasion. He accepted a commission to write it for the tenth centenary of the Protestant Augsburg Conference and it was first performed in London in 1830 and then Berlin in the same year, but never in Augsburg because of Catholic opposition. It is entitled the *Reformation Symphony* but he hated this symphony but was persuaded not to destroy it. It is an exuberant work that deserves attentive listening. Mendelssohn's first movement theme—(now the *Dresden Amen* of the Saxon Liturgy)—was used by Wagner as the *Grail* theme in his opera *Parsifal*. The last movement introduces the very popular tune since adopted for the Lutheran Chorale *Ein Feste Burg**.

The same theme was also used for a popular Christian hymn. Wagner was so impressed by the Symphony's skilful and beautiful construction that he adapted some of the themes for his *Parsifal* opera.

Meyerbeer also made use of the last movement theme from Mendelssohn's Dresden Amen in his opera *The Huguenots*.

Mr. Mendelssohn had earlier composed his *Ave Maria* which was such a sacred and beautiful version that it caused many to convert to the Roman Catholic faith. *Ave Maria*, and Mozart's *Ave Verum Corpus,* are also regarded by many to be the most sacred music in existence.

However, when Mendelssohn accepted the commission to write the *Reformation Symphony* he fell out of favour with the Roman Catholic Church and the performance of any of his music was firmly discouraged—but often conveniently attributed to the 'traditional' at Christmas when his carols are sung and at weddings when his weddings march is played.

Mozart suffered the same fate for becoming a Freemason but was forgiven and his music rehabilitated by the then Pope in June 1985.

---

*   a safe stronghold

It is also in the final strains of Mendelssohn's *Reformation Symphony* that we hear the beginnings of that other popular carol *Christians Awake, Salute the Happy Morn.*

There was a period when all was quiet and nothing much creative was being produced when Mr. Mendelssohn, quite out of the blue, gave the world his *Violin Concerto* and since its first performance it has remained a firm favourite of both virtuosi and audience alongside the other three great violin concertos of Beethoven, Bruch, and Brahms. Mendelssohn's two piano concertos in G Minor and D Minor are also firm favourites but perhaps mildly lacking the technical ostentation of the later Mozart piano concertos.

Mr. Mendelssohn was Europe's leading pianist and organist in his day being continuously engaged for concert performances. Wherever he appeared, either as instrumentalist or conductor, theatres and concert halls were filled to capacity and he had to put a stop to the continuous encores, a practice prevalent in those days.

Married to Jean Marie, a French girl whom he met on one of his many visits to Paris, they had four children and one of his greatest pleasures was to play the piano to them. They were intent listeners. In the course of these musical sessions he produced a series of piano pieces entitled *Songs without Words* and another series *Songs my Mother taught me*. Two of these songs he especially dedicated to his little ones, namely the *Spinning Song* and the *Bees Wedding Song*. Many of these beloved 'songs' are nowadays part of piano tuition exercises.

Of his three well-known overtures, *The Hebrides* is perhaps the most popular and its descriptive mood contrasts sharply with that of *Calm Seas and Prosperous Voyage*, whereas *Ruy Blas* his tribute to his friend Victor Hugo's play of the same name, is not particularly exciting. Impressed with the ruggedness of the Hebrides islands and particularly *Fingals Cave*, Mendelssohn experienced the 'salt air', rough seas and sea gulls' of the area that inspired him into a most popular and descriptive piece. He sketched the overture whilst on the Island of Staffa in the Hebrides and completed it at Burnham Beeches in Buckinghamshire. He would sit on his favourite bench, under the Beech trees, each day working on the *Hebrides Overture*. The bench still stands in Burnham Beeches as a memorial to him. Compare the whinny of horses in Wagner's *Ride of the Valkyries*—a later work of Wagner's—to the high wind effect in Mendelssohn *Hebrides Overture. Calm Seas and Prosperous Voyage* reflects the impression the bay of Naples had on the composer.

Mr. Mendelssohn composed many other works and only a handful have been discussed here, but we must not overlook his three great oratorios, *Christus, St. Paul* and *Elijah*. The latter is considered to be a work of truly divine inspiration and beauty—the tunes of many of our popular hymns have been adapted from it—whereas *St. Paul* portrays his own missionary zeal—to promote the works of the 'greats' and bring the enjoyment of beautiful music to ordinary people. He composed a large number of songs with lyrics, many of which are still popular today.

Some three years before his death Mr. Mendelssohn was commissioned by the King of Prussia to enlarge the overture to *Midsummer Night's Dream*. Having a lifelong fascination for Shakespeare's comedy of that same title he gladly accepted and there soon followed the beautiful incidental music—about twenty years after the overture. It too was immediately successful throughout the world. Later converted into a ballet. Shakespeare's comedy, complemented by Mr. Mendelssohn's music, remains a constant favourite amongst audiences and is considered to be a most delightful short ballet.

One wonders if Rimsky Korsakov received orchestral inspiration for *The Flight of the Bumble Bee* from the opening bars of *you Spotted Snakes*. Compare the music. It is in the music of Mendelssohn's *Dream* that Shakespeare's characters Titania, Oberon, Puck and the braying Bottom (the donkey) come to life. The fairyland effect is brilliant.

Mr. Mendelssohn was a handsome, cheerful and most genial man. He was tall and slim with a shock of curly black hair. He was meticulous in everything he did. His musical scores and letters to friends and family are works of art in themselves. He was always popular with audiences and endowed with a most modest disposition and constantly regarded others to be his betters. Among his other achievements was the setting up of the Leipzig Conservatory, one of the world's leading musical institutions even to the present day. He encouraged and persuaded both Robert Schumann and Chopin in their careers giving financial help when needed. The man was a workaholic—tirelessly striving to bring the enjoyment of music to all people. To this extent he helped and encouraged Charles Halle to set up the now famous Halle Orchestra. He had few enemies—always ready to help others whenever he could.

In 1846 Mr. Mendelssohn returned from a concert tour of England after learning of the death of his beloved sister Fanny. He suffered a stroke through overwork and depression, from which he partially recovered, but he would not rest. Unable to compose or arrange concerts he turned his hand to his other gift—painting in watercolours. He set about mounting an exhibition of his paintings in Paris, the proceeds from which would go towards arranging concerts for new works by Schumann and Chopin. Alas, he did not live to see the successful outcome of this venture for he suffered another stroke and died on the fourth of November, 1846, at the age of thirty seven.

So ended the life of another child prodigy but, unlike Mozart, whose funeral cortege was supposedly attended by only a stray dog, Mr. Mendelssohn's was attended by a huge crowd. There were many dignitaries from all over Europe among the mourners. The Leipzig conservatory turned out in full. One of his last acts was to co-operate with Robert Schumann to arrange a concert at the Gwendhaus in Leipzig for the sole purpose of giving the first performance of Schubert's C Major Symphony (The Great

Symphony) which Mendelssohn conducted himself before it had even been published and after ten years of it lying dormant. It was a huge success and, if it had not been for Mendelssohn and Robert Schumann, Schubert's work may have been lost to the world, together with many of his other works.

A life completely fulfilled was ended of one to whom we shall be forever grateful—one who spent most of it striving to bring the enjoyment of music to us all—not only his music, by any means—but also the music of others. This widely gifted man—this bourgeois genius—the complete musician—would have succeeded in anything he attempted, whatever his social or financial status, had he not succeeded in music.

* * *

Mendelssohn-Bartholdy—Felix is the Latin word for 'happy'—was much more than a polite composer with an enormous technique. His music has sensitivity, style and a great degree of personality. He did compose at least one flawless specimen in each of the musical forms, symphony, concerto, piano, chamber music, fugue, the lied (song), the concert overture, and oratorio. Everything indeed—except opera. His influence can be found in the music of Gounod, Faure, Richard Strauss and Tchaikovsky. His music is once again being accepted and he is being recognized as the sweet, pure, perfectly proportioned master he was—and a most happy person.

PLAY ON MR MENDELSSOHN—DO PLAY ON.

THE END

The Wedding

For Jennifer and Simon

Thank goodness this did not happen on your special day.

James Lord was about to marry Jo' Hippy and all arrangements had been made at St. Woden's Roman Catholic Church with full nuptial mass. The reception was to be held in 'Island Hall' a building adjacent to the church. All plans had been organized smoothly, including the pealing of the Church bells. James (Jamie) was somewhat disappointed that the bells could not be tuned to play his favourite *Seventy Six Trombones* from the popular musical show *The Music Man*.

The bride's dress, veil and bouquet of flowers were all in place, so too was Jamie's hired penguin suit—black tie and tails—with pin-striped grey trousers and close fitting top hat to complete his wedding attire.

Jamie was a fireman of some nine years experience based at the local fire station. He shared a 'two up', 'two down', house with his fiancé Jo'. Jo' occupied the upstairs and Jamie the downstairs where he slept on a camp bed when not on duty. They shared the bathroom and kitchen and this arrangement was to continue until they were married. Both were staunch Roman Catholics.

Jamie became a bit of a nuisance a few weeks preceding the wedding by continuously asking his colleagues what type of rings did they think he should buy. They became so fed up that they began to refer to him as *Lord of the Rings* (J.R.R. Tolkein's book).

Jo' worked at the local hospital as a nurse. This was the profession chosen by her at her graduation. Her current duties were in the operating theatre and it was her responsibility to ensure that all the surgical instruments were sterilized and other paraphernalia kept spotlessly clean. This entailed cleaning the kidney dishes and sharpening scalpels on grindstones and the smooth oil stones so that all were in pristine condition and the scalpels sharp. Jo' was popular with her fellow medical staff and was always referred to as Missus Hippy (or Mississippi).

On the morning of their wedding that was to take place at 11.30 am that day, both Jo' and Jamie began their day with slight problems. Jamie ignored the alarm clock and nearly overslept. In making a dash for the kitchen so that he could wash and shave at the kitchen sink, as was his custom since Jo' and he decided to share the house, and being in a sleepy state he bumped into what they prized as their piece of Chippendale furniture (bought in kit form from the now defunct MFJ Furniture Company). However, his wash and shave restored him to full consciousness and he recalled the poem of A.E. HOUSMAN contained in his anthology of poems *A Shropshire Lad*:

> Yonder see the morning blink
> The sun is up and up must I,
> To wash and dress and eat and drink
> And work and God knows why.
> How often have I washed and dressed
> And what's to show for all my pain,
> Let me lie abed and rest

> Ten thousand times I've done my best
> And all's to do again!
>
> *A.E. HOUSMAN*

Fortunately he did not cut himself shaving because he very quickly realized that this was his wedding day and henceforth he would be able to complete his morning ablutions in their bathroom and not in the company of the microwave, etc.

Meanwhile, Jo' was busy upstairs getting herself ready for their wedding. The door bell rang and a partly dressed Jamie ushered in Donna, Jo's close friend, who had come to help Jo' arrange her hair and put the tiara on it, help Jo' don her wedding dress and any last minute things that a bride might need to be done in preparation for her marriage. Jamie directed Donna upstairs to where Jo' could be found. After sometime and now fully dressed in her white wedding gown, Jo' discovered that an age-old custom was now called for as the bride should wear *something old, something new, something borrowed and something blue.*

"What can we do about that Donna?" Jo' asked.

"Well, it's quite simple really. Your wedding dress is **new** and you **borrowed** your white shoes off nurse Eileen. Your veil is going to be fixed with some **blue** plastic coated paper clips, but as for something old—well, let us think for a minute—do you have an old garter?"

"No, I haven't. I never wear garters", replied Jo'.

"Well leave it to me. I'll go and see if I can find something—like a piece of old elastic or something", and off Donna trotted down the stairs and out through the front door. Her bright idea paid off as she soon found a large, broad, red rubber band that had been used to secure one of his bundles of mail and had been dropped by a postman. Donna hurried back to Jo' who quickly slipped the rubber band on to her left ankle to complete the customary **old** requirement.

All was now ready. Jamie had taken their car to the church as Jo' would be travelling with her father, Ted, in a wedding car decorated with white ribbon.

Jamie was waiting patiently in the first pew in front of the altar for Jo's arrival and, when he heard some slight shuffling and whispers at the entrance to the church, he knew that his bride had arrived.

The organist commissioned to play at the wedding struck up the music somewhat resoundingly whilst Jo', with her hand resting on her father's arm, walked with him slowly to join the bridegroom at the altar. However, the organist seemed to be in a bit of a jumble because she began to play the *Wedding March* from Felix Mendelssohn's incidental music for *A Midsummer Night's Dream*, that is 'Here Comes the Bride and Bridegroom'. After the couple had made their marriage vows and signed the register in the presence of the priest, deacon, two witnesses and an approved person—this was a Roman Catholic wedding requirement—the bride and groom slowly walked back down the aisle towards the door and this time to the organ strains of Richard Wagner's *Wedding Music* from his opera *Lohengrin*—'Here Comes the Bride'. The two important pieces of music had been played at the incorrect stages of the ceremony. At the door Jo' and Jamie were greeted by the deacon who shook their hands and congratulated them on their big event and wished them every happiness in their future life together. He introduced him self as Paul Postlethwaite and then said to Jamie,

"I'm sorry, I didn't quite catch your surname".

"I'm Jamie Lord, son of Zebedee and your name is Paul. Could you please tell me whether St. Paul ever received any replies to his letters to the Corinthians or Thessalonians?" Quite taken aback with this question the deacon could only answer by saying,

"I don't really know but I will try and find out for you".

"Thank you", replied Jamie.

Bride and Groom then proceeded to the steps of the church to have their customary wedding photographs taken by the photographer and others among the guests who had taken along their cameras to capture the moment.

It had been pre-arranged by Jamie's colleagues at the fire station that the bride and groom would be transported in one of the fire engines, accompanied by three members of his regular crew, around the streets for half a mile before returning to the reception hall adjacent to the church. A very fine and apt gesture indeed so Jamie and Jo' climbed into the cab followed by two other firemen, Paddy O'Hooleran and Cecil Surtee. They set off on their 'round the block' trip but had only driven about two hundred yards when Jack Moseley, the driver, received a call from the fire station supervisor directing them to a small furniture warehouse on the Tadcaster Road. Jack explained that they had just attended Jamie's wedding but was told that was of no avail as this was an emergency. Fortunately the firemen's protective clothing and helmets were in the cab. There was always a spare helmet too in the cab. Jack told the others of the situation, asked them to get ready promptly and with klaxons blaring drove swiftly to the furniture warehouse that was by now well and truly ablaze. Another fire engine and crew, supervised by George Henderson, were already at the scene. The crew of the fire engine that Jamie and Jo' were, by this time, in the protective clothing complete with helmets. Jamie used the spare helmet and joined them, but without protective clothing, whilst Jo' alighted from the fire engine and stood watching from the front of the truck her bouquet firmly gripped with both hands.

The fire was soon practically dowsed when George came over to Jack and said, "Jamie is improperly dressed for attending a fire. He's dashing around like a penguin with a tin hat!"

"Yea, we've just come away from his wedding", replied Jack.

"Well, I hope he took his protein pills before putting his helmet on, (from David Bowie's *Space Oddity*), retorted George sarcastically.

Jack then spotted Jo' standing by the fire engine dressed in her wedding gown but he did not associate her presence with Jamie's wedding and, misunderstanding the situation, went over to Jo' and said, "It's very good of you lass for coming along so soon and so solemnly and beautifully dressed to lay a posy of flowers at this site but I'm afraid you're a little premature as we haven't yet established whether there are any fatalities. You had better go home and await any later news about this fire. If there are any fatal casualties you can then bring your posy to lay at the site". Jo' felt too disgusted to respond.

Now that the fire was extinguished Jamie and his bride, together with his pals, proceeded to drive in the fire engine to the reception hall. In their rather long absence the best man, another member of Jamie's crew, Fred Hatchet, kept the guests occupied with banter and silly small talk. Fred was good at this and was often referred to as the 'hatchet man'.

When the wedding group arrived at the reception hall grounds they all jumped out of the fire engine cab and removed their protective clothing and helmets. All were slightly stained with ash and smoke streaks, including the bride. Paddy O'Hooleran, on removing his protective gear shivered slightly.

"Are you cold Paddy?" enquired Jack.

"Only a bit—I had some water go down the back of my neck", he replied.

"You know what Confucius would say", answered Jack and went on, "**Hoolie, hoolie, you are foolie, you should always wear a woolie**'".

"For goodness sake shut up Jack", scolded Paddy.

The group then entered the reception hall—ushered in by the 'hatchet man'. There was a rather pungent odour enveloping the hall. Jamie, who was extremely partial to 'Bombay Duck' (a stick-like fish, salted and dried and eaten as an accompaniment to curries), was delighted. "The caterers were thoughtful", he thought.

After the speeches and reading of the congratulatory cards, etc., was over the guests were advised to start helping themselves to the buffet style fare laid out on the tables. The Bombay duck and a bowl of curry was then brought in and laid on the table. The pungent smell in the hall was caused through the freshly fried Bombay duck in the adjoining kitchen. The deacon, who was an invited guest, felt he ought to bless the offending Bombay duck to perhaps alleviate the smell. Jamie immediately helped himself to curry, purees, bajis, poppadoms, mango chutney, and, of course, his favourite fried fish Bombay duck. Any leftovers of his favourite he planned to take with him, suitably wrapped, on his honeymoon.

Fred Hatchet approached Jamie to tell him he was out of cigarettes and that he would go to the nearest shop to buy some. Jamie acquiesced and when he returned Jamie said to Fred,

"Did you get some cigarettes?"

"Oh yea, thanks", and went on to add, "While I was waiting to be served I heard a bit of the news on the newsagent's radio in the background. There wasn't much on the news except that another holiday company AIR SOL had gone into administration.

"Did you say AIR SOL?" queried Jamie rather surprisingly.

"Yea—I'm sure it was AIR SOL—why are you so concerned?"

"Because if it is AIR SOL then it means our honeymoon arrangements are right up the creek. We have booked two weeks holiday in Istanbul. I had better 'phone them on my mobile and confirm what you have said is correct". You are not winding me up are you?"

"No mate, certainly not", stressed Fred.

Jamie stepped outside and using his mobile telephone confirmed that AIR SOL had now gone into administration and therefore all holiday bookings had been cancelled. Further information would be supplied later.

Rather dejected he re-entered the reception and found that the festivities were ending. He did not as yet impart his knowledge regarding AIR SOL to his bride Jo'.

It was time for them to leave and their guests were assembling outside to witness their departure. Jamie and Jo' then emerged from the hall and stood together hand in hand on the top step. Jamie thanked his guests for attending their wedding and for the smashing wedding presents and wished them all well. The crowd cheered and clapped and Jo' clutching her bouquet threw it into the crowd very excitedly. Unfortunately her throw was quite fierce and off target and the bouquet went flying over the six-foot brick perimeter wall and into the neighbouring garden. Jo' was quite embarrassed. They then made their way to Jamie's car with shoes and rice being thrown, by some members of the crowd, in place of confetti. The rice was, however, taken from a pack of a well-known brand of 'Rice Crispies' cereal, and the two pairs of shoes were worn out old firemen's boots.

On the way to their destination Jamie stopped the car, in a quiet lay-by, and revealed the bad news to Jo' who, very astounded, dejected and irate, said, "Trust b—AEROSOL to let us down! What do we do now?"

"Well, firstly you are very polite to call the company AEROSOL. I would call them something stronger. Let's just go home and think about what we are going to do now", replied Jamie.

"It will take us a couple of days for us to sort this out and plan another honeymoon destination", responded Jo'. If we do as you suggest we will need to go shopping because most of our food, especially fresh food, has been reduced because we were going away my love".

"Okay, on our way home we pass a supermarket. Let's go in there and do some shoplifting and take it home', suggested Jamie.

"Shoplifting? We would get caught", Jo' laughed. "We don't want to spend our honeymoon in police custody".

This they did, that is the shopping—not the shoplifting-and Jo' did not look too prominent as before going into the supermarket she had donned a summer-ware black knee length coat after removing her ash stained veil. Normally the bride and groom would have gone home to change into their 'going away' outfits and would have returned to the hall to say goodbye to their guests but because of the fire emergency and the AIR SOL fiasco, their plans were disrupted.

Shopping now completed and after struggling to rescue some of the items, after a wheel on the shopping trolley collapsed, they got into the car and seated themselves comfortably.

"I wish you hadn't brought the left-over Bombay duck with you from the reception. It smells absolutely horrid—in fact the car stinks of it and will for some time no doubt", Jo' said to Jamie. "Never mind, no doubt we'll survive, the nasty odour will clear a little if we let the windows down. Let's go home now!"

HOME JAMES AND DON'T SPARE THE HORSES!

THE END

Hammer & Sickle

In memory of the late Ronnie Barker and the unveiling of his statue in the grounds of the new Waterside Theatre, Aylesbury, Buckinghamshire, October 2010.

*

The Author has no knowledge of the secret services but has attempted to write this espionage tale from pure imagination.

*I*n 1984, the year that the author *George Orwell* predicted that it would be the one where the world would be faced with *Armageddon* both the Soviet Union and the nations of the West, led by the United States, were acting belligerently towards one another. There was stepped up sabre rattling by both the Warsaw Pact countries and the West. The Soviet Union was extremely concerned about the progress the west was making in the development of new weaponry. The West was equally concerned about the progress the Soviet Union was making in the field of destructive weaponry.

Edward (Ted) Benton, an established agent at MI6 was a man of average weight and height who had gained a reputation as a trustworthy, dedicated, individual by his superiors. He was a man aged forty-seven who started his career as a police constable on the beat and who then transferred to CID as a detective constable. Thereafter, when the opportunity arose he applied for and was accepted, after several security checks and a thorough assessment of his character, into the secret service. Since he was self-taught, fluent in German and the Baltic languages, his first assignments were carried out in these countries and in particular Berlin. He was nearing completion of eleven years with the secret service. Ten Benton was a single man and lived alone in a rented apartment in West London. He was extremely conscientious in his work and very rarely fraternized with other agents, his colleagues. In fact, for very obvious reasons, agents were strongly discouraged from doing so lest they be recognised by other foreign secret agents if they worked or mixed socially. They were all strongly advised to act independently and alone and have as few acquaintances as possible. In fact he had made it known to his widowed mother that he worked for the insurance industry. Their superiors or handlers only ever interviewed the agents when they were to be updated, or given new assignments, or the latest information concerning their quest. Otherwise they were left to pursue their task alone unless it was absolutely necessary to group them in twos or threes if the assignment required additional agents.

Ted Benton received a communication that he was urgently required to attend a meeting with his superior, Douglas Watson, who was in sole charge of a section that organized a group of agents in espionage activities. Ted was instructed to discontinue his current surveillance task and to meet Doug Watson in his office at headquarters. Ted of course wondered what the emergency was all about and duly attended as instructed. After initially updating his boss on his present assignment situation Doug Watson went on to brief him on his new and very important assignment.

"Now then Ted, what I am about to tell you is very hush-hush and you must not breathe a word about it to anyone. The job will entail some stalking", advised Doug. "There is a laboratory that is named CFN

IVERSON (Electronic and Technical) that ostensibly researches and develops garden weed-killers and fertilisers, and it has been working on producing a mass destructive weapon using a laser beam bounced off a geo-satellite to destroy and completely obliterate a target or targets on the ground, with devastating effects. The organization has been working on this project for some years and has finally worked out a rather complicated formula in the process to eventual success. However, unfortunately, it is convinced that the formula has been acquired by a person, or persons, unknown and clandestinely passed over to an agent, or agents, of the Soviet Union, the KGB. They have therefore sought our help in trapping such persons and of course doing so will be very much in the national interest. I would like you to engage in this assignment as top priority and on this basis I have arranged for you, accompanied by agent Tom Brooks, to visit the laboratory on the pretence that you are both interested in their new fertiliser product".

Ted understood the explanation and agreed to do as requested. Doug Watson then went on to tell Ted that when he and Tom make their visit the laboratory they would be introduced to some of the technicians and scientists. One of the characters needed careful scrutiny, also that the person to whom he referred was quite extrovert and often acted accordingly by not only shaking hands with a person to whom he was being introduced, but also has the habit of tapping the introduced person on the upper arm as though it was his greatest pleasure to be meet the stranger.

"He is the person most suspected of espionage", explained Doug. "I would advise that you follow his movements diligently. Report back to me in due course, or leave it to me to call you back for an update".

"Okay sir, I'll see what I can turn up", replied Ted.

And so Ted began stalking his quarry, known as Mr. X. Four days later Ted followed Mr. X down to the underground trains at Leicester Square station. There on the platform was Mr. X, sat on a bench rolling a roll-up cigarette from a tobacco tin. It was not long before a Mr. Y joined Mr. X and, after greeting one another Mr. X passed his tobacco tin to Mr. Y who promptly began hand rolling a cigarette too. From where he was standing (quite close to them) Ted noticed a loose cigarette paper in the tobacco tin. Both had rolled cigarettes with a view to smoking them when they emerged from the underground. Soon they both stood up, Mr. X to board the train for Heathrow airport whilst Mr. Y headed towards the exit of Leicester Square station. In departing they hastily reiterated, within earshot of Ted, that their next meeting was to be held at the Toad & Stool public house in Uxbridge at eight o'clock on the following Sunday evening. However, when Mr. Y went on his way he mistakenly left the tobacco tin on the bench where he and Mr. X had been sitting. When Mr. Y was out of sight Ted quickly grabbed the tin, opened it and found the loose cigarette paper on which appeared to be a formula, or part of one, scribbled on it. He immediately extracted it and discreetly put the cigarette paper in his jacket pocket and placed the tin back on the bench. He had no sooner done this when Mr. Y came running down the platform to retrieve the tin and proceeded again to leave Leicester Square Station.

Several minutes before the appointed time on the following Sunday Ted arrived at the Toad & Stool public house in Uxbridge. He wandered into the saloon bar, ordered a drink of best bitter beer and sat at a table to enjoy it. Some minutes had elapsed when Mr. Y arrived and ordered a drink at the bar then he, too, sat at a vacant table and began to enjoy his drink. Very soon Mr. X joined him at his table. Mr. Y greeted Mr. X then bought the latter a drink. Mr. X who seemed to slightly recognize Ted, having met him on Ted's visit to CFN Laboratories and then at the underground station nodded to Ted who returned the gesture. Apart from Messrs. X and Y and, of course Ted, there were two men sitting at a table drinking and busily engaged in some serious conversation. There was also a mixed group of eight sat at another table in a corner of the saloon bar, again, drinking and enjoying banter. Otherwise the saloon was practically empty for a Sunday night.

After a short while Mr. X and Mr. Y proceeded to exit the saloon to enter the small outdoor patio fitted with an awning for those who wished to have a cigarette, as smoking was not permitted in the saloon bar. Messrs X and Y left their half full pint glasses and a newspaper on the table. Ted strolled out into the pub garden and stood near X and Y whilst he took his own tobacco tin from his pocket to hand roll a cigarette but, at the same time, watching every action Mr. X and Mr. Y were about to make and, as Mr. X was about to pass a loose leaf paper to Mr. Y, Ted immediately stepped in and asked if they would be kind enough to let him have a cigarette paper, pretending that he had run out of papers, from Mr. X who immediately obliged by offering him the pack of papers. Ted declined the packet and firmly said he was quite happy to have the paper Mr. X was about to hand to Mr. Y. Very reluctantly the loose paper was handed over to Ted. Scribbled on it were some letters and figures. He then turned to both X and Y and informed them that he was a government agent and produced his warrant card to substantiate his position. He then accused them of espionage and advised them to remain on the patio and at the same time signalled to the two men sitting together at one of the tables. Immediately they left their drinks and joined Ted. They advised Mr. X and Mr. Y that they were Detective Inspector Geoff Coley and Detective Constable Greg Wick. D.I. Coley asked X and Y what their names were. Mr. Y was George Coulter and Mr X was Ken Allsop.

"Mr. Coulter and Mr. Allsop you are both under arrest and I will now caution you both. Have you anything to say?" stated D.I. Coley. "We will handcuff you both and take you to the police station for further questioning and investigation. Mr. Benton would you follow us to the station with the evidence you possess?" requested D.I. Coley. Thus they all headed for the police station.

On their arrival Ted Benton spent a few moments jotting down notes in his notebook. Inside the building Ted handed over the two cigarette papers, on which were the incriminating details of the alleged offence supposedly committed by Coulter and Allsop, then thanked the police officers for their cooperation and left the building. He was not required to remain there during the questioning of the two suspects. In fact it was Ted who had arranged for the police officers to be present that evening at the Toad and Stool public house as he strongly suspected some form of handover of information from one suspect to the other bearing in mind their brief words on parting at the underground station platform a few days earlier.

Ted was very pleased and satisfied with himself having stalked and eventually assisted in cracking yet another probable spy ring. He would 'phone his lady friend and treat her to an evening meal sometime during the coming week to celebrate the occasion. This he did as soon as he arrived at his apartment and an arrangement was made for them to meet on the following Tuesday evening.

Nine days later Ted received a call from his headquarters telling him that his boss Douglas Watson would like to see him in his office at 10.30 a.m. for what he expected to be a thorough debriefing about his last successful assignment. After Ted had parked his car he had to walk, through a severe sleet storm, from the parking lot to the office building. The age-old adage entered his mind.

Galosh-less-ness is foolishness when sharply slants the sleet.

Ted wished that he possessed a pair of galoshes as his shoes were squelching.

Ted Benton entered the office and was welcomed by Doug Watson. He was, however, surprised to see sat along the wall near to Doug's desk D.I Geoff Coley and D.C. Greg Wicks. Douglas Watson then offered Ted a seat in front of his desk and a mug of coffee, and, of course, reminded him that he had already had the pleasure of meeting the two police officers at the close of his last assignment. Doug explained that their presence was in response to their request to attend the debriefing because they were both seriously thinking of applying for a transfer to the secret service. He also explained that they were keen to get some idea of the work and procedures of the service and that a debriefing of a secret service agent was a good place to start unless, of course, Ted had objections to their being present. Ted did not demur and settled himself in his chair and made himself comfortable.

"Ted, I am very pleased with your latest result, just as I am pleased with all the progress you made in your assignments when you were in West Berlin and the Baltic States. Thank you for all the hard and tricky work you carried out", said Douglas, and Ted was very appreciative of his comments. "Now, let me turn to a matter or matters of much more importance, but first there are a few points about yourself I would like to clear up and perhaps you could enlighten me", continued Doug.

"I'll do my best so please fire away", replied Ted.

"Well, to begin with, do you live alone?"

"Yes, I do. I have an apartment here in Demford as you already know", responded Ted.

"Yes I did but I just want all details to be absolutely clear, so please bear with me", advised Doug.

"Do you do much cooking or baking for yourself, or do you eat out most of the time?"

"No, I don't do any real cooking. I don't have the time or inclination what with the sort of work in which we are engaged. I mostly have snacks or visit restaurants or eat ready-prepared food like fish and chips and so on".

"Yes, I assumed so—just as I used to do when I was engaged in 'field work'. So, what would you do if somebody gave you, say, a goodly amount of Bramley cooking apples—or other fruit suitable mainly for cooking".

"Well, if there was sufficient I should accept them gratefully and take them to my parents who live at Hinkley which, as you know, is quite near", replied Ted. "My mother enjoys cooking and would bake me an apple pie, or apple crumble, to take back to consume in my own apartment".

"I would do the same if I were in your shoes", Doug said. "To continue, whilst we are on the subject of food, do you ever dine out of an evening—and I don't mean just for a snack and if so do you dine out alone or do you have the company of a friend or acquaintance?" asked Doug.

"Yes I do occasionally dine out and whilst I have been in England I have had the pleasure of dining out with a lady friend, but I must quickly add she is only a lady friend and no more".

"Good, that's fair enough", replied a satisfied Doug.

At this stage Ted was quite bemused at the turn the discussion was taking and could not see the relevance of these questions.

"Now tell me", continued Doug, "are you a gambling man?"

"Yes, in so far as I have some bets on horse racing from time to time. I'm afraid it's one of my vices. The other being that I am a smoker and I roll my own cigarettes out of a tin of cigarette tobacco".

"Do you have many worthwhile wins on the horses or are you a complete loser?"

"I have had some winners but not that many. I do it for a bit of fun mostly and not to get rich quickly, if you understand what I mean".

"Yes, I do", responded Doug, "and do you use the same bookmakers or do you dot around others", Doug asked.

"I use the same, mostly Ernest and Baileys, the bookmakers just down the road from this building. They have a good reputation and they provide a good, friendly service".

"Yes, I've heard that they are good from others, although I don't gamble myself", explained Doug.

Ted was now beginning to get a little bit agitated and began to feel uncomfortable. Again, he could not understand the relevance of all of this in connection with his last assignment. Nevertheless Doug had not finished and continued further.

"Let me now turn to the thrust of this interview, or debriefing as you have been led to believe, and what this is really about. Firstly, the cigarette papers handled by the two men Ken Allsop and George Coulter was just a ruse. They are both special agents and were acting under my direction".

"Hang on", interjected Ted, "you directed me to follow and stalk Ken Allsop after noting his appearance after my first encounter with him at the CFN Laboratories, and this I did".

"That is correct", replied Doug, "but it was all arranged. Let me explain. The scribbling on the cigarette papers that you took into your possession and copied on to a piece of paper before handing them over to the police, represented a false formula. The names of the two culprits were false and so was their arrest by these two police officers. You were handed a bag full of cooking apples by a man whom you would tell us was a snout, an informant, but in fact he was a secret Russian agent and at the handover you passed him a piece of paper on which was copied the formulae from the cigarette papers. You were seen placing the bag in the boot of your car. Then you drove to the mall area, locked your car and proceeded to enter a restaurant for a meal. While you were in the restaurant two of our agents who had borrowed, with the full cooperation of the nearby Vauxhall dealers, a bunch of car skeleton keys to enter the boot of your Vauxhall Viva and extract the bag of apples. When you returned to your apartment you very surprised to find the bag was missing and you desperately searched places you had previously been to that morning thinking you may have mislaid the bag somewhere.

Ted Benton was now shocked with the information that had just been disclosed and quickly tried to explain. "The piece of paper I handed over was a racing tip and the apples were a gesture of appreciation".

"Some gesture", continued Doug. "When we opened the bag, buried underneath the apples, we found a bundle of money in wads amounting to over two thousand pounds. What do you say to that?"

"That was winnings on a horse racing bet", explained Ted.

"Really, so you get your informant to place bets for you, do you?"

"Sometimes, yes", replied Ted.

"I don't believe you—your informant's name is Michail Vishniski and he is currently under arrest and in custody.

Ted was absolutely flabbergasted with the information he had just been given.

"I will continue", said Doug. "With the aid of the Police Financial Investigation Unit and the cooperation of the manager at Burton's Bank, that is your bank and branch, your account has been scrutinized and there are entries of rather large deposits made over several months. Where did this money come from?"

"My winnings on horse racing bets. I do accumulation bets and I have been quite lucky over these months", replied a very agitated Ted.

"This is not so because we have checked out the bookmakers Ernest and Baileys and they tell me that it is very rare for them to pay out such large sums of money. We showed them a picture of you but nobody in the establishment, although they vaguely remember you as a punter, has ever paid you a large sum of money in respect of a winning racing bet. So that explanation will not be acceptable. I say to you that these sums of money have been paid to you from time to time by your 'so called snout' for information you have passed over. Now let me explain something else to you. Your lady friend, whom you join for dinner on occasions, is Olga Tyler and she works for CFN Laboratories and at these dinner meetings she has been passing secret information on technical developments to you and, in turn, you have passed the information to your Russian friend for a financial reward. Am I right?" asked Doug. "You obviously share the proceeds with Olga Tyler. Well you may be interested to know that Olga Tyler is also under arrest and in police custody. Also, the information she has passed to you has all been false because she too has been a suspect for some time and detailed information, false of course, has over these last few months been deliberately put in her way by CFN Laboratories, knowing that she would filch them" continued Doug.

Ted Benton now began to bluster and burst forth with various reasons for the large deposits entered into his bank account, also stated that he did not know that Olga Tyler worked for CFN Laboratories. He knew that his explanations were not acceptable to Douglas Watson and that he had been truly entrapped. Doug Watson then continued,

"I am very disappointed in you Ted because in the past you have done some very good work for our organization, both here in Britain and abroad and I cannot understand why, or what made you turn traitor. You have let us all down and had we not suspected you in the very beginning you would have most certainly jeopardized the security of our country. I shall be discussing this sorry episode with you again very soon but, in the meantime, these two police officers are not present here to witness a debriefing, as I said earlier, but to arrest you and charge you with espionage. You may have gathered that this is an offence for which you will go to prison. Your only consolation is that you will perhaps be safely locked up and out of the way of any retribution that may be visited upon you by the Soviet secret service for passing to them false information over several months for reward". Turning to the two police officers Doug said, "Well, inspector and constable you can now take him away but I hope to see you both soon when I come down to the station or prison, pending his trial, to interview him further.

Ted Benton was duly handcuffed and taken away by the policemen, closing the office door as they left.

Doug Watson stretched back into his chair feeling quite satisfied but sad at the outcome. He immediately thought of the spy sketch he had recently seen in a BBC TV sitcom. In it a British secret agent was given the task of spying on a Russian couple, believed to be spies. The actor* was sitting in

---

* *The actor who played the part of the British secret agent was the late Ronnie Barker.*

an apartment overlooking and opposite to the apartment that the couple occupied. Through his binoculars he saw the couple arrive, go upstairs to their apartment where they switched on the lights leaving the curtains open. They immediately began fondling one another. After a while the woman went to their kitchen and then brought out a small plate of sandwiches. After the sandwiches had been eaten the woman returned to the kitchen and brought out 'wotsits' on two small plates. The actor playing the part of the British secret agent could not make out what the 'wotsits' were on the plates but kept his binoculars trained on the couple. After the couple had demolished the 'wotsits' they drew their curtains. The secret agent, codenamed PILGRIM, could see no more through his binoculars but nevertheless he was obliged to report his progress, and exactly what he had seen, to headquarters by using the apartment telephone, but in a coded form.

In the circumstances all he could think of was as follows:

Hammer and sickle
Slap and tickle
Cheese and Pickle
Bubble and squeak!

A wry smile crossed Doug Watson's face. He then drank the cold remains of his coffee, closed his file, locked it in his desk drawer and departed the office.

THE END

The Refuse Man

This story has an element of truth in it but all characters are fictitious.

He had been working as a refuse collector since leaving school with no qualifications. His late father and mother advised him to take on the refuse job and Ian Hill followed their advice and did just that and had been in the job for some twenty-seven years. He was now aged forty-three and living alone in Attenbury. Ian was employed by the local council until the council subcontracted out the refuse work and he continued to work for the subcontractor with the same arrangement as he had with the council regarding remuneration, pension contributions, rights, and hours to be worked. The subcontractor also allowed the former working practises and allotted areas of refuse collection to continue as it was considered pointless to rearrange the current efficient arrangement.

Ian Hill was one of a crew of three, sometimes four, when the collection load was at its greatest, such as Christmas for example. The other members of the crew were Mark Davis, the refuse collection wagon driver and bin man Nick Adams. The three were close colleagues and had themselves devised their own system in order to carry out the work quickly. At the time of the unfortunate incident that occurred Mark Davis was nearing retirement whereas both Ian Hill and Nick Adams still had many years of working life before they could retire. They were a happy, jovial trio and often helpful to householders. There were of course other crews like them.

'Bin-men', as they were sometimes called, were regarded by some as 'those who lacked intelligence' and did not have an acceptable standard of education', and some were regarded as 'retarded'. This was quite wrong and insulting because, although the job was menial and repetitive, their work was of the greatest importance and absolutely necessary. Much more important than some jobs that required the worker to sit in front of a computer monitor tapping keys on a keyboard. They also had to face the constant changeable weather conditions, but they enjoyed working outdoors. They needed to be physically robust. There was one occasion when Ian Hill was approached by a burly man, (a clever dick), who asked him,

"What's it like being retarded?"

"That's funny", responded Ian, "I was going to ask you the same question".

The perpetrator of the insult hit Ian on the head with his ring-encrusted fist. Ian did not retaliate.

Ian was a kind, helpful individual whose main interest was football. He supported Tottenham Hotspur and keenly followed their fortunes, and misfortunes, through the press, television and radio. Ian remembered that when he first started on the job bin-men, as they were called in those days, were required to lift and lug metal or plastic dustbins for emptying into the bin-wagon and then return the bins to their respective households. This method of collection was replaced by the use of black plastic bags, issued by the council, for householders to put refuse in for collection. It had its advantages in so far as there was no necessity for the bin-men to make a double journey to and from properties. The introduction of the wheelie-bin system lightened the load but, after mechanically emptying the wheelie-bin, the workers had to return the bins near to the householders' properties. Refuse men receive only average wages and no other emoluments. It is only at Christmas that a few householders treat them to tips or cans of beer, wine, or boxes of chocolates that they share out amongst themselves. The vast majority of householders completely ignore them and the very essential work they do. They are treated as though they are there to automatically provide a service paid for through council taxes, often forgetting that underneath each yellow-coated reflective safety coat there is a human being with feelings and intelligence that most often goes unnoticed. Ian Hill and his colleagues were such people. Ian had a reputation, by those who knew him, of being a mild man full of kindness and helpfulness. If a householder on his round forgot or missed placing the bin out for collection, Ian would attempt to put the matter right. The crew with whom Ian worked had a system in their areas of collection whereby Ian would proceed ahead of the bin-wagon and gather the wheelie-bins into groups so that when Nick Adams and Mark Davis came along with the wagon the bins were emptied without the wagon having to stop, perhaps every two minutes, outside every householders' property. Sometimes Ian would be approximately fifteen minutes ahead of his colleagues and would, as soon as he was joined by the wagon, help the others with putting the wheelie-bins onto the platform of the wagon and returning them to households after the bins were emptied. It was on such a occasion that an unfortunate incident occurred.

Ian had reached an area, where the houses were surrounded by a green and where he began assembling the wheelie-bins for collection, when a four-year old girl ran out of her front door and up the tarmac path. The little girl fell, grazed her kneecaps and began yelling. She was still down on her knees when Ian immediately ran over to her, picked her up and then sat her down on a tree-bench on the green. The child kept on crying and to try and calm her he took a clean tissue from his pocket and wiped the blood from her kneecaps and, as the girl was in a state of shock, he put his arm around her to comfort her to stop her crying. The girl's mother came running out of the house, very agitated, and ran over to them. She immediately, without asking for an explanation, snatched the child away and falsely accused Ian of pushing over the girl with a wheelie-bin and then molesting her. Ian tried desperately to explain what had happened but the hoity-toity mother refused to accept his explanation. She then took the child back into the house and Ian carried on assembling the bins. Very soon a police car arrived—and so did the bin-wagon—and two policemen started questioning Ian about the incident. He had been reported for pushing and molesting a child. His explanation of what had really happened was of no avail and he was taken to the police station where he was charged with the offence. Some weeks later Ian was in the dock of Attenbury Magistrates Court on trial. The solicitor who had been allocated through the legal aid system, after discussing the facts with Ian, advised him to plead guilty to the offence of molesting a minor because, if he pleaded not-guilty, the magistrates would probe his actions, especially in light of the convincing evidence proffered by the child's mother, as the four-year old could only speak a few jumbled incoherent words, and he could end up in prison. This Ian did and was given a suspended prison sentence of three months. Ian was now free from the worry of the likelihood of a prison sentence hanging over him but he was quite concerned by the fact that his name would be entered onto the paedophile register. Ian was not a paedophile. His case was then reported in the weekly local newspaper. This report caused a very nasty backlash from the local yobbish characters. They daubed his house, bequeathed to him, as an only child, by his parents when they died, with the word PAEDOPHILE and other offensive expletives in GRAFFITI form.

This was by no means the end of the matter because, very soon after his trial, his employer called him into his office and told him that his services were no longer required. He was dismissed. He not only lost his job but, under the company rules, his pension rights—towards which he had contributed for many years—too were foreclosed. These events devastated Ian and it took him quite a while to accept the consequences. He soon forced himself to face the unfortunate facts and move on. He was a man of very strong character. He soon found another job, rather more menial and less demanding than that of a refuse collector, and was paid a lower wage. His new job involved keeping tidy, clean, and trim, the hedges and shrubs surrounding an area for parking and loading area to a row of large mixed shops—a shopping mall. He was, on the whole, left to get on with the job without constant supervision. Periodically his work was checked and found to be faultless.

However, to add to his woes, his devoted friend and work colleague, Mark Davis, was killed in a road accident caused through an out-of-control car driven by a drunken yob. This incident left Ian shattered as, ironically, some three weeks earlier, his other bin-man colleague, Nick Adams, was imprisoned for being over the limit at the wheel of a vehicle. It was not the first time that he had been caught driving whilst under the influence of alcohol. Both Ian and Mark had warned Nick of the consequences but Nick always thought he knew when he should not have another drink that would tip him over the edge. Now it was too late for further warnings. These events caused the break-up of a long-standing friendly relationship and Ian's thoughts turned to sadness and to a few lines he had read in a church newsletter.

By these methods we may learn wisdom:

First, by reflection,
Which is noblest;
Second, by imitation,
Which is easier; and
Third by experience,
Which is the bitterest.
CONFUCIUS

It was lunchtime and it was Ian's routine to sit on one of the benches under the trees to eat his sandwiches and drink coffee from his small flask, both prepared and brought from home. In inclement weather he would sit in the small tool shed at the corner of the yard and have his refreshments. He was slowly sipping his coffee when his thoughts turned to his best friend Mark Davis. He remembered fondly how for many years Mark quite routinely brought to work a large flask of ground, percolated, coffee prepared by his good wife. He always shared this with Ian and Nick, his workmates, whilst on the bin-collection round. This was always very welcome and refreshing to them when they were out in all types of weather and Ian and Nick were most grateful for the kindness and occasionally donated towards the cost of the coffee beans. They also referred to Mark as the *GUNGA DIN of the coffee pot.* Having remembered Mark and his nickname he began saying to himself some of the lines from *RUDYARD KIPLING'S* moving poem about a loyal Indian water carrier who moved amongst the soldiers offering them water from his goat-skin water bag during battles and skirmishes against Afghan tribesmen in the hot, hostile North West frontier region of India during the reign of Queen Victoria. It was Ian's favourite poem and he fully appreciated what *Kipling* was trying to convey to his readers and the British establishment. The salient lines of the poem are:

You may talk of gin and beer
When you're quartered safe out 'ere
An' you're sent to penny-fights and Aldershot it;
But when it comes to slaughter
You will do your work on water,
An' you'll lick the bloomin' boots of 'im that's got it.
Now in Injia's sunny clime,
Where I used to spend my time
A servin' of 'er Majesty the queen,

Of all the black faced crew
The finest man I knew
Was our regimental bhisti GUNGA DIN.

For a piece of twisty rag
An' a goatskin water bag
Was all the field equipment 'e could find

And for all his dirty 'ide
'E was white, clear white, inside
When 'e went to tend the wounded under fire.

I shan't forgit the night
When I dropped be'ind the fight
With a bullet where my belt-plate shou'd 'a' been
I was chokin' mad with thirst
An' the man that spied me first
Was our good old grinning, gruntin' GUNGA DIN.
'E lifted up my 'ead
An' plugged me where I bled,
An' 'e guv me 'arf-a-pint o' water green
It was crawlin' and it stunk,
But of all the drinks I've drunk
I'm gratefullest for the one from GUNGA DIN.

'E carried me away
To where a dooley lay,
An' a bullet came an' drilled the beggar clean
'E put me safe inside
An' just before 'e died,
I 'ope you liked your drink, says GUNGA DIN.

So I'll meet 'im later on
At the place where 'e has gone—
Where it's always double drill an' no canteen;
'E'll be squattin' on the coals
Givin' drink to poor damned souls,
An' I'll get a swig in hell from GUNGA DIN!
YES, DIN! DIN! DIN!
You lazarushian-leather GUNGA DIN
Though I belted you and flayed you,
By the living Gawd that made you
You're a better man than I am GUNGA DIN.

This is not the full poem. These lines are excerpts from RUDYARD KIPLING'S BARRACK-ROOM BALLADS.

In remembering lines from this poem Ian wondered whether Mark Davis would now be squatting on the coals giving a drink of his delicious coffee to poor damned souls. No doubt he would, because Mark was a very kind and thoughtful soul.

As Ian was putting his empty flask away in his knapsack he spotted an old friend walking towards him across the yard. It was Benny Johns whom they frequently met while emptying wheelie bins. Benny owned and ran a small thriving company called *'Wheelie Clean'* and used to follow the refuse men on their rounds in order to clean the bins for the householders who paid for this service, hence he became one of the trio's best pals. Ian particularly liked the Wheelie Clean logo.

HAPPINESS IS A CLEAN WHEELIE BIN.

THE END

Sherlock Homes

The author has deliberately spelt HOMES this way, as you will see if you read on!

Detective Sergeant Neil Spencer was quietly and comfortably sat on the bench in the cemetery, some one hundred yards from the main entrance, enjoying his lunch-time sandwiches and coffee from a small flask when the sky above him darkened slightly and a buzzing noise could be heard above in the sky. It was a 'murmuration' of easily five hundred-odd starlings. He looked up and saw the birds pass over. He enjoyed watching starlings, especially at eventide when a murmuration of them would perform wonderful aerobatics for all to see. He also enjoyed walking along the cemetery footpaths to watch squirrels darting in and out the gravestones and scooting up the trees. He also enjoyed the charms of finches fluttering amongst the variety of trees growing in the cemetery grounds. He often spent his lunch break in these surroundings when weather permitted, when he was working at the Police Station that was opposite the cemetery gates, rather than in the small rest room at the station.

After completing his lunch break Neil returned to the station and entered the small office where he worked and which he shared with Detective Inspector Reginald (Reggie) Crabbe. Neil Spencer had served over twelve years with the police force—seven years as a constable and four years as a plain-clothes detective. He enjoyed the work and was able to put some of his talent to good use. He was conscientious, very observant, and had a unique sense of recall. Being single was also an advantage as in, his job, as detective, he was often required to work long hours. He lived in a maisonette locally, in Duttsford (twinned with *Kill your Speed!*) His colleague, Reggie Crabbe, was also a conscientious officer with greater experience of police detection work. He was a quiet, thoughtful, perfectionist, individual. They both shared a close and friendly relationship. Neil had on several occasions met D.I. Crabbe's wife and two young teenage children—a daughter and a son. Of course, in their work they often had differences of opinion and approach. This was bound to happen but on the whole they worked well and very successfully together.

Reggie Crabbe greeted Neil Spencer with the usual perfunctory words and asked him to sit down, leave the work he was doing and to listen carefully. He then explained, "We have been notified of a missing person from her bungalow, situated in the rather exclusive area Imber Park, here in Duttsford. Do you know it Neil?"

"Yes, I do, but I am not totally acquainted with every part of the area", replied D.S. Spencer.

"Well, to continue, this missing person, a Mrs Alice Tusker, is rather a frail eighty-seven year old widow who lives alone and, according to close neighbours, rarely goes anywhere, even to a local shop, without advising her next door neighbour. Officers from uniform branch have already questioned her neighbours but none can throw any light on her disappearance. Alice has been missing for three days and her next-door neighbour, whom she entrusted with a spare bunch of keys, allowed the officers to enter and search all around her dwelling to see if there were any clues as to her whereabouts. They came up with nothing positive. In fact it is very strange, as it was explained to the officers, that her wheelie bin was placed outside the property in the usual spot only yesterday morning in readiness for the refuse collection. This morning it had been returned to where she usually keeps it, near her back garden gate. However, the large black plastic bag, that Alice Tusker always used to line her wheelie bin to keep it clean, was not put into it. Since she has been reported missing, uniform branch find it very strange that someone should have dealt with her wheelie bin. Neighbours have been questioned about this but none admit to doing it. They have, however, said that last week there was a young male tidying up her garden and other gardens in the area and, apparently he is still working in the area. Officers have been asked to find him and bring him in for questioning. No body has yet been found and there are no reports of a body being found anywhere in the surrounding area, or even further afield from home. That's it in a nutshell. We have therefore been asked by the super' to take over the case."

"Well, where do we begin?" asked D.S. Spencer.

"I've no idea—but we can start with interviewing the young gardener chap when he is has been located and brought in", responded D.I. Crabbe. "He might be able to give us some answers. It seems, to begin with, that this is a case of abduction. However, as yet, no ransom has been demanded and if this were the case the abductors would not receive much, as she doesn't appear to be very wealthy, although the lady was sitting on quite an expensive property, but to realize income from its sale would take months, as you well know".

The young gardener was located and brought to the police station and said his name was Tony Hubbard. He was not able to give the officers any helpful information and only said that he had done some garden work for Alice Tusker for which she paid him thirty pounds and gave him a mug of tea plus a cupcake. The police officers felt that there was no reason whatsoever to suspect wrongdoing by Tony Hubbard and duly ended the interview. He was then released. They had to find another means of getting to the bottom of this incident. It was an absolute puzzle—where were they to begin. Pictures of Mrs Tusker, taken from her bungalow were reprinted and circulated and also published on television but as yet to no avail.

D.I. Reggie Crabbe suggested that Neil should visit her close neighbour. Mrs Ivy Brunton and see if there was anything, even titbit information from her and her husband, that might be of help in solving Alice Tusker's disappearance. Ivy Brunton explained to D.S. Spencer that they were very close friends and that she, Ivy, accepted freely the responsibility of taking care of Alice without being too intrusive. Ivy also explained that her only living relative was a nephew who was a solicitor working at Digby and Randalls, a partnership firm of solicitors, quite near to the estate. It was also revealed that the nephew only visited his aunt Alice very occasionally because—and it was only her impression—they did not get on very well with each other. It would appear that his visits were probably regarded, by him, and made as a duty call.

The officer asked, "Is it possible that Alice was taken to a hospital as an emergency case?"

"Certainly not", replied Ivy, "because I have already telephoned four hospitals in our district and they have no record of any emergency admission from Alice's house and I can assure you that if Alice was going, or being taken somewhere, she would let me know by some means or other. She knows I would be extremely worried otherwise".

"Thank you Mrs Brunton, this information will be of help to us", said D.S. Spencer". He then returned to his office to report back to D.I. Crabbe.

The following day Neil Spencer went to the cemetery and his favourite bench to sit and enjoy his sandwich lunch and flask of coffee. Some twenty yards in front of him there had been a burial and three of the cemetery workmen were just completing their job of filling in the grave and building a mound of fresh soil and shingle. He was quite impressed at the respectful way in which they arranged the wreaths and bunches of flowers on the mound before pegging in a small number tag at the head of the mound. They then removed boards of plywood, or hardboard, from the edges of the grave and carried them away. The mound of soil on the grave was quite low and not the usual size, so the person interred must be a youngster he thought. Neil finished his sandwiches and coffee and, as he got up to stroll through the pathways, he let off a loud roaring noise by passing wind. He laughed to himself, apologized to the startled squirrels and birds and immediately thought of a rather humorous poem about the Duke and Duchess of Gormley Moore who were invited to attend a 'posh' banquet at the invitation of the portly Earl of Grumditch. It was after the meal and whilst they were sipping the remains of their wine, when

All of a sudden the Duchess broke wind
It was really awfully loud
But she wasn't going to admit it was her
She was high born and dreadfully proud
So she turned to the footman behind her chair
"Stop that", came her voice like a blow
"Certainly M'lady", he smartly replied,
"Which way did it go?"

Contributed by a member of the
BRITISH KOREAN VETERANS ASSOCIATION

Neil Spencer sat down again because he spotted a rather smartly dressed man coming along the path doing some jottings in a notebook. He acknowledged Neil by nodding. He then seemed to study the newly filled in grave opposite Neil before proceeding down to the main gate and along the stone wall and past the part of the wall that had been knocked down. The gap in the wall left an unauthorized entry to the cemetery. The man then disappeared out of sight behind the trees and shrubs. Neil returned to the station to continue his work.

The next day, when he returned to his favourite cemetery bench to have his lunch, he noticed something odd and different to the grave of the very recent burial that lay opposite to where he was sat. After he had eaten his lunch he walked the few paces to the graveside to examine it. He found that the mound on the grave was much larger than it had been the previous day, the flowers and wreaths were positioned a little haphazardly and there were remains of fresh soil on the grass verge that surrounded the grave. To satisfy his curiosity he sought out the three workmen having their break in a hut in the cemetery grounds and in a friendly tone questioned them. They followed him to the grave in question and after examining it they assured him that since filling it in they had not in any way disturbed it. They pointed out that they would always use boards if they removed any of the soil, which was extremely rare after such a recent burial, and agreed that fresh soil remains were certainly present on the grass edges now. They agreed that the mound was definitely larger, also the floral tributes had been rearranged, quite possibly by the deceased relatives or friends.

When D.S. Spencer returned to the office he gave D.I. Crabbe a full explanation and expressed his deep concern and foreboding. D.I. Crabbe respected Neil Spencer's observations and advised him to find out from the register of births, deaths and marriages, the name and address of the interred individual's next of kin and seek their permission to have the grave reopened. D.I. Crabbe impressed upon him that he had to stress, strongly, the urgency of obtaining their permission to proceed. Within three days they were given the authority they sought.

D.I. Crabbe and D.S. Spencer accompanied by two uniformed policemen and with the help of the cemetery workmen opened up the grave. They had dug down some two feet when they discovered a large plastic bag containing the body of an elderly woman. D.I. Spencer immediately called for forensic examination and for the coroner's services. Both were expeditious and the body was removed to the mortuary at the local hospital for identification and post mortem examination. D.I. Crabbe was extremely praiseworthy of D.S. Spencer's powers of observation. Identification would now pose a problem. D.S. Spencer suggested asking Mrs Tusker's neighbour and close friend, Ivy Brunton, to offer her services to help identify the body. This Ivy reluctantly agreed to do, when the body was revealed to her, she identified it as that of Alice Tusker, the missing person. However, it was necessary for a member of the Tusker's family to confirm the identification and Ivy Brunton suggested they seek out the nephew who worked at Digby and Randalls solicitors, situated quite near to their estate. Ivy knew of no other relatives. Nor did she know the nephew's name because Alice Tusker very rarely referred to him or even saw him.

D.S. Spencer paid a visit to the firm of solicitors and, not knowing who he was looking for, rather sheepishly, asked if any member of the establishment had mentioned anything about a missing relative. One of the firms secretaries quickly confirmed that one solicitor by the name of Brian Potts had told them that it was his aunt that had been reported missing in the recent media publicity. D.S. Spencer asked if he could speak to Potts and after questioning him about his aunt Potts confirmed that it was his aunt who had been reported missing. Brian Potts was then requested by the Detective to accompany him to the coroner to positively identify the remains. He agreed to do so and showed surprise that his aunt's body had been found in the cemetery of all places.

"By the way, was it you I saw walking through the cemetery the other day jotting notes in a notepad. Am I right?" asked D.S. Spencer.

"Yes, it was", he replied, and added, "two disabled pensioners are suing the Highways and Byways department of the local council for the state of disrepair to the cemetery pathways, because they find it difficult to negotiate their mobile wheelchairs along the paths. I am handling their case and under their instructions have already issued a writ. I was just examining the pathways and making some notes".

"Oh, I see", responded D.S. Spencer.

Thereafter Brian Potts positively identified the body as being that of his aunt, Alice Tusker.

The report from the coroner's office clearly stated that Mrs Tusker had been murdered, the perpetrator, or perpetrators, having strangled her but DNA evidence was sparse because the murderer must have used surgical gloves and crept up on her from behind because there was no sign of bruising to suggest a struggle by the unfortunate woman. D.S. Spencer suggested to D.I. Crabbe that perhaps they should begin by interviewing the solicitor Brian Potts as it would appear he had a possible motive for the killing. D.I. Crabbe agreed and suggested her neighbours' should also be questioned. However, before doing so it would be wise to check with the Highways and Byways council department whether a writ against them had in the meantime been issued. The officers did this and after extensive enquiries at the council offices discovered that the council had received no writ regarding the cemetery pathways. Armed with this information they then returned to the solicitor's offices to question Brian Potts. He did confirm that his aunt had made a will and testament over a year ago and had taken his advice and lodged it with the firm of Digby and Randalls for safekeeping and enactment when the time arose. After some rigmarole and pressure on the part of the two police officers who were investigating the murder, they stressed that they had every right in requesting to see the will prior to its being read after the funeral.

Alice Tusker's will revealed that her only living relative, Brian Potts, would inherit both her bungalow and her savings in the bank, which amounted to quite a tidy sum, also a building society savings account—in fact her whole estate, apart from two small amounts of money she had bequeathed to her favourite charities. He was the only beneficiary. Brian Potts was then asked to accompany the police officers to the station for interview and questioning.

After asking Brian Potts whether he would like another solicitor present for the duration of the questioning, Brian Potts responded by saying that he was quite capable, as an established solicitor, of handling the questioning himself.

D.S. Spencer began by saying, "You advised me that you had issued a writ against the Council for disrepair of cemetery footpaths, didn't you?"

"Yes, I did", he replied.

"Well, I'm afraid we have made extensive enquiries at the council offices and cannot find any trace of a writ being issued. They deny all knowledge of one. What have you to say to that?"

"They must have mislaid it, or lost it", he emphasized and turned quite pale.

"I don't believe that an important matter of a writ would be lost by them, or even mislaid", responded D.S. Spencer. "There was no writ, was there?" asked the police officer.

"Well, there will be one soon", responded Brian Potts.

"That's not the same as emphasizing one had already been issued", retorted Spencer.

"To continue, are you a gambling man Mr. Potts?"

"No, I'm not", answered Potts.

"Are you thinking of moving house sometime in the future?"

"As a matter of fact we are thinking of moving to a more select area in due course, provided we have the money", he replied. "We may even move into my aunt's bungalow once her will has been enacted".

The police had already taken a DNA swab off Brian Potts for testing but with little hope of positive identification, because some DNA evidence would already be available at Mrs Tusker's dwelling, as Brian Potts had visited her albeit on rare occasions.

"Let me now divulge to you my suspicions", said D.S. Spencer. Turning to D.I. Crabbe he asked, "would you object sir if I proceed?"

"No, not at all, just carry on—I'm listening", affirmed his boss.

"Now Mr. Potts, your aunt was a very quiet, respectful and reserved woman, her only friends and associates were her neighbours. She was certainly not abducted, nor was a ransom demanded and besides, who would do this not knowing anything about her financial affairs. Therefore, as I see it—and I stand to be corrected, you murdered her and placed her body in a black wheelie bin liner before putting her body in the boot of your car ready for disposal. You strangled her whilst wearing surgical gloves so that you did not leave any fingerprints. You then awaited the opportunity to dispose of her body. You very cleverly decided to bury her body on top of a recently interred body. When I saw you in the cemetery you were noting a suitable new grave for your purpose and later went back during the night—when all was quiet and although the gates were locked you gained access through the gap in the broken wall—complete with shovel and a powerful lamp, removed all the wreaths and floral tributes, removed the top soil and dug down some two feet and placed your aunt's bagged body on top of the recently interred body. You then refilled the hole, returned the wreaths and flowers. However, the mound was greater than it had been after the initial burial. Also you left traces of fresh soil on both sides of the grave. The cemetery workmen assure me that they always use boarding when digging out or replacing soil into the graves. Also, there is no writ issued by you, or your firm, to the council. You are the only person, apart from a couple of charities, who will benefit from her demise. What have you to say to that?"

"I think you have got it all wrong and I resent your accusation", replied Brian Potts, rather forcefully.

"Nevertheless, Mr. Potts I am charging you with the murder of your aunt, Mrs Alice Tusker".

Mr. Potts was cautioned and taken into custody pending trial for murder. D.I. Crabbe was quite astounded and so pleased with D.S. Spencer's power of observation and perception, and the precise manner in which he conducted the interview. He offered to take Spencer to the pub to buy him a pint of his favourite beer and a bite to eat. Whilst drinking their beer and eating their snacks D.I. Crabbe said to D.S. Spencer, "Who would believe that a reputable solicitor would lower himself to commit murder and very cleverly dispose of the body".

"Well, Reggie, it takes all sorts to make a world".

A smile then crossed D.I. Crabbe's face and he asked Neil Spencer whether he had heard the story of the schoolteacher and her class of pupils. Spencer had not so Crabbe said he would tell it to him.

A schoolteacher decided to break some of the monotony of the day by asking every pupil the same question, 'what work their parents did for a living'. After responses from several of those in her class, she came to young Jimmy.

"What does your father do Jimmy?"

"My dad is a lorry driver Miss".

"Does your mother go out to work Jimmy?"

"Yes, she does", he replied. "She goes out soliciting every day from nine to five".

"Soliciting every day", responded the teacher astonishingly.

"Yes, she's soliciting every day and sometimes on a Saturday. If she is sick or on holiday she does not go soliciting", affirmed Jimmy.

"How strange", replied the teacher.

The teacher had not comprehended the fact that Jimmy's mother was a solicitor!!"

The two detectives had a good laugh at the tale and D.I. Reggie Crabbe said to D.S. Neil Spencer, "that estate where the late Mrs Tusker lives is quite select and exclusive isn't it".

"Yes it is", replied D.S. Spencer. "I believe it was built by a firm of building contractors named **SHERLOCK HOMES**.

THE END

The Reverend

For Don, a good friend, and his faithful canine companion Rosie.

It was a dark October evening when Reverend Fredrick Cooper was sat quietly in his small Spartan sitting room jotting his thoughts on a piece of paper that would form the basis of his Sunday sermon at mass. At the ripe old age of eighty three Father Fred, as he was known throughout the parish and beyond, had long since passed retirement age but he had been asked consistently to continue as parish priest by the Bishop of the diocese because of the acute shortage of replacements. He always obliged because he loved being the resident priest of St. Xavier's Roman Catholic Church that served a mixed community. His small church could only ever accommodate a small congregation of about one hundred people when filled to capacity. It was an old church, and badly in need of redecoration when church funds permitted and to achieve this aim Fr. Fred lead a rather frugal existence. However, he was on very friendly terms with his opposite numbers in the reformed churches in their small town. He had been parish priest at St. Xavier's church (Xavier being the patron of all missions) for nearly twenty years and, apart from ladies of the congregation who cleaned and decked the church with flowers, he was helped by three much younger men who took responsibility for counting and banking church donations, opening and locking up the church building each day and other necessary work. He was always most grateful for their assistance.

Fr. Fred was a mild man full of kindness and was often approached by his lowly parishioners for advice and the divulgence of their personal and family problems. He was a good listener and was regarded as somewhat forthright but sincere in his replies and statements because he relied on his many years of experience in any advice he proffered. Nevertheless he was a likeable man who would never short shrift anyone who approached him. He had spent all his life as a parish priest at other parishes and also a three-year stint in the Army Chaplains' Department stationed at Tel El Kabir, an army base alongside the Suez Canal in Egypt, when he was a young man. He did, however, care for the homeless and when sufficient provisions of tinned food and other items of food and clothing were donated by parishioners, he would go around the town, Norbury (twinned with SLOW DOWN) distributing the donations to the homeless holed up in shop doorways and other recesses. They were extremely grateful to him.

At just after eight o'clock Fr. Fred decided to lock his door and to repair to bed after having a mug of weak cocoa. Before doing so he stepped outside in the dark to grab a breath of fresh air. An Owl flew above him as he did so. It was quite strange. He had never seen a parliament of owls nor for that matter a murder of crows. He had only ever seen the odd owl or two, or three crows feeding together. He locked up and proceeded to make a mug of cocoa. Just then there was a knock on his door. He was rather startled and wondered whether he was being called out to administer the last rites to a dying person. When he opened the door he was confronted with two young men. They were wearing black balaclavas under hoods. They forced their way in passed Fr. Fred, hitting him with a truncheon type weapon across his back as they did so.

Fr. Fred was absolutely shocked with the intrusion. The villains demanded money from him. He explained that he had no personal money apart from some small change that he had left on his hall table. They then, swearing and using foul expletives, hit him twice at the back of his head before throwing him to the floor. They dragged him up off the floor, hit him several times again with the truncheon and pushed him into his chair. He explained that the only money available was that from the morning collections taken at the two Sunday masses that day and locked in the safe. It amounted to only £188. They forced him to open the safe and give them the money that the fabric bag contained. This he did and before departing they assaulted him again with the truncheon. Fr. Fred was in absolute shock but was able to telephone the police. When the police arrived Fr. Fred gave them a complete account of the incident but they immediately sent for an ambulance to take him to hospital. At the Accident and Emergency department nurses dressed the wounds to the back of the priests head and those inflicted on his back, administered some medication then advised him to return to his quarters and rest for a few days because he was concussed. There was no need for his assailants to beat him so viciously because he had not put up any resistance. He was a kind, quiet man. Feeling quite disorientated and distraught he went to bed without his drink of cocoa. At the masses he celebrated during that week the small regular congregation noticed that his behaviour was somewhat irregular but knew not the reason.

The following Sunday, when Fr. Fred was at the altar celebrating mass, he noticed two young men standing at the back of the church. Throughout the service they stood still and completely upright like two sentries on duty. After the service they promptly left. On several occasions some odd persons, mainly latecomers, would stand at the back of the church but they participated by kneeling and genuflecting at the appropriate times during and after the service. But the two young men were obviously non-Roman catholic.

The following Tuesday evening there was a knock on the door and when Fr. Fred opened it he was surprised to see the two young men standing outside. One was clutching a plastic carrier bag and it appeared they wanted to see him.

"Good evening—how can I help you?" he asked.

"Mister, we have something to say to you and to ask you", they replied.

"Well do come in out of the cold", was his response. "What was it you wished to see me about?" Fr. Fred queried.

"Well, its like this", one of the lads replied. "We have come to ask you for your forgiveness".

"Forgiveness, what have you done?" questioned Fr. Fred.

"We were the lads who beat you up and robbed you a couple of weeks ago and we now ask for your forgiveness", they replied and added that they had visited the church to see him the previous Sunday morning but he was busy at the altar.

"Oh, I see", said Fr. Fred and continued by saying, "I have already forgiven you—straight after the incident. You two should really ask God to forgive you, not me, and by the way my title is not Mister but Father".

"But where is God?" asked one of the lads.

"God is standing right beside you—he stands right beside each one of us. If you are really seeking forgiveness ask God here and now to forgive you and say that you are sorry. He will surely forgive you if you are sincere", stated Fr. Fred.

After a few moments silence they handed the priest the plastic bag that contained a cotton bag, tied up with string. It contained the money they had robbed from him. They assured him that not a penny of the money had been touched or spent or even counted. Fr. Fred was quite astonished with the turn of events. He then advised them to report the incident to the police and that they would no doubt be charged with robbery and violent behaviour but they would have to face the consequences. Before they departed they agreed to do as the priest requested. Whilst bidding them farewell and before locking the door, Fr. Fred stepped outside and noticed a heavy frost was beginning to settle. He immediately thought of that old adage:

If the frosts of November can support a duck
The rest of the winter will be slush and muck.

Three weeks later, early Tuesday evening, there was again a knock on the door and Fr. Fred, who was engaged with another young visitor at the time, opened the door to find the two young men who had attacked him standing there again. They said that they had called on him to see how he was getting on. He invited them in for a chat and asked their names. One was Joshua (Josh) Cole and the other was Andrew (Andy) Stickland. He then shook hands with them and explained that his young visitor Darren Gross had only popped in to say hello as he had accompanied his father, Roy Gross, who had come to lock up the church for the night and that he was on his way home now with his dad. The priest explained that Darren had just recited a sad little ditty to him about the birds and asked him to repeat it to Josh and Andy. Darren promptly but shyly repeated the poem.

Poor little dickybirds
Poor little things
Out there, in the cold, cold, night
Their heads tucked under their wings.
Anon.

They all thought this ditty was wonderful and very true. Darren then left to join his dad. Fr. Fred remembered and told them about an adage he had recently seen emblazoned on a sundial in a parishioner's garden. It read

> *Time wastes our body and our wits*
> *But we waste time, so we are quits.*

The lads thought how true this was too.

The priest then invited them to sit down and offered the lads a mug of tea each After the tea was handed out to them and they began sipping it, he proceeded to ask questions in order to get them to participate in friendly conversation. He asked whether they had, on his advice, reported to the police. He knew that they had done this because the police had 'phoned Fr. Fred who confirmed that, as the money they had robbed from him had been returned and that the lads had apologized profusely for their wrongdoing, he would not be pressing charges against them. Josh and Andy confirmed that they had done so and that they had been severely cautioned by the police. Fr. Fred was delighted to hear this and told them so.

During the conversation that followed the priest was told by Josh and Andy that they were two orphan boys who had worked on building sites as labourers since leaving school. They had no academic qualifications and had become bored so they decided to resort to burglary and robbery as 'easy pickings' and that Fr. Fred was the first victim.

"You were bored?" queried Fr. Fred. "I cannot understand this attitude at all because there is so much of interest in life and so much each one of us can do to help others. It always astounds me when I hear youngsters say that they are bored and yet when you visit their homes and see their gardens they are full of discarded toys, books, electronic games, etc., all thrown aside when the novelty has worn off. Of course adults are just as bad. We seem to have developed a culture of 'I want, I want, I'll get', with no mention of 'I'll do, I'll give'. Although I must stress that many, many individuals do things, some wonderful things to help others and they are most generous. What are you lads going to do now? Go back to the building sites? You have both very courageously, responsibly and manfully accepted the consequences of your wrongdoing and repented. Please don't let it go to waste", advised Fr. Fred. "Tell me, what have you lads been doing since we last met? Let me first say though that I think both of you are well educated. Am I right?"

"Well, we left school without any qualifications. We had to work for a living and to pay for our digs. We continue to not have much money so cannot contemplate associating or socializing with girls as much as we would wish", replied Andy.

"What were your favourite subjects at school?" queried Fr. Fred.

"My favourite was General Science and Andy's was History", responded Josh.

"General Science and History"—I see. Are you good at History Andy?"

"Oh, he is very good. He can even name all the kings and queens of England in proper sequence", said Josh.

"Ah, that's only because I rely on the aid of a poem, taught to us at school, otherwise I wouldn't be able to remember", Andy responded.

"Can you recite the poem to me now because I'm very interested?" requested Fr. Fred.

"Yea, sure, but first I must warn you that some names are in slang form so that they rhyme, such as Willy means William, Harry is Henry, Stee is Stephen, Dick is Richard, Ned is Edward, Bess or Bessie is Elizabeth.

Majestic Verse

Willy, Willy, Harry, Stee, Harry, Dick, John,
Harry three, one two three Neds,
Richard two, Henry four, five, six, then who,
Edward four, five
Dick the bad
Harries twain and Ned the lad.
Mary, Bessie, James the vain.

> *Charley, Charley then James again.*
> *William & Mary, Anna Gloria, four Georges,*
> *William & Victoria, Ned, George, Ned,*
> *George then a Bess.*
> *May our kings and queens be blessed!*

"That is very good", exclaimed Fr. Fred. "Will you write that out for me so that I may pass it on to a history teacher in one of our schools"

"Of course I will", Andy replied obligingly.

"Now let us get back to the question I asked earlier—what have you been doing since we last met?" asked Fr. Fred.

They explained to Fr. Fred that, since they last met him, they had cleared their wrongdoing with the police and, with the aid of a small bank loan in addition to their savings, they had bought a small second hand pick-up truck. Their friend Kevin, a mechanic, had checked it thoroughly and carried out some minor repairs that had cost them a few pounds. They were now in business as general handymen. Kevin had stencilled the name **'JOSH AND STICK'** and mobile telephone number on the cab doors. Since then they had attracted many customers for jobs to be carried out on private properties, mainly because their rates charged were extremely reasonable. They were building a clientele of regular customers and their business had progressed rapidly in a short space of time. They both enjoyed the variety of work and were reliable hard workers.

Fr. Fred was delighted to hear this because, unbeknown to them, he had prayed for them and God had answered his prayers. He then asked whether they had done any work at an area flooded recently when the river on the outskirts of the town flooded the properties on its banks. They assured him that they had but that there was more to do.

Fr. Fred then explained, "you know, in these days of modern technology, I cannot understand why some large manufacturer of double glazed windows and doors cannot produce waterproof versions since waterproof doors for front loading washing machines and walk-in baths have been in existence for some time, so why not do the same for windows and doors? In areas prone to flooding waterproof doors and windows would be an absolute boon".

"True, but what about air bricks near the footage of the walls of houses—water would seep in through the air bricks?" asked Josh.

"Well, one suggestion would be to devise a fixed frame around the air brick to which the property owner or tenant could attach a temporary waterproof cover. Surely this could be done", replied Fr. Fred.

"Why don't you write to some firms and suggest this Fr. Fred?" responded Andy.

"I wrote a letter to the *Daily Chronicle*—a quality newspaper—suggesting this but they did not countenance publishing it", replied Fr. Fred and continued, "but then I suppose I'm only a simple priest".

The lads were surprised to hear this but could not offer any constructive suggestions even though they thought that his ideas were feasible.

"Anyway, my friends what you must continue to do is to persevere to build up your small business. Remember Rome wasn't built in a day. You will need a whole lot of patience and you must strive to overcome any setbacks. As the saying goes, *patience is a virtue and virtue is a grace and Grace is a little girl who would not wash her face.*

Fr. Fred and Josh and Andy continued chatting and discussing a variety of subjects. Andy asked Fr. Fred whether he had heard the one about a religious lad who approached his parish priest and very solemnly asked,

'Father, is it alright to smoke while I am praying?"

'Good Lord, no! Certainly not! That would be a mortal sin—but you can pray whilst you are smoking', said the priest.

They all chuckled. Fr. Fred then quoted a philosophical quotation from Voltaire: **Shun idleness. It is rust that attaches itself to the most brilliant metals.**

It was time for them to say their farewells and Josh said, "We'll come and see you again father as long as you don't try to convert us".

"I would love to see you lads again—anytime—and I certainly would not attempt to convert you or anyone else. That is something for the individual to decide but you both will always be very welcome here", said Fr. Fred.

"Thank you Fr. Fred and good night", and with those words they all stepped outside the door—Fr. Fred to look at the stars as it was a clear night sky and the lads to make their way back to their lodgings.

The two lads fully accepted the **'rust'** philosophy and referred to it on several occasions. Two days later after they had visited Fr. Fred, during a lunch break, Josh and Andy had parked their truck in a long-stay, free, car park. In the process of crossing the road at a properly controlled pedestrian crossing, on the way to buy sandwiches from a cafeteria, a car came speeding down the road and crashed into them. The force of the impact caused them to be flung against the pedestrian crossing post and bounced them on to the edge of the pavement. The car, driven by a tearaway, ignorant, low life driver, sped away rapidly. An ambulance was called immediately, also the police who called for witnesses. Josh and Andy were taken to hospital. Both were diagnosed with concussion and several other injuries but, fortunately, no broken bones. They were detained in hospital with the possibility of being kept there for at least a week.

The accident had taken place quite near to St. Xavier's Church and some two days after the hit and run Fr. Fred heard about it and that it had involved the two young men, Josh and Andy. Fr. Fred decided to visit them in hospital as he did with any of his parishioners that were in hospital even though it meant a walk of three quarters of a mile for him. He didn't have a car at his age and he did not mind the walk except in inclement weather. When he arrived at the hospital he was directed to Ward H on the third floor. Unfortunately he had an aversion to elevators and lifts so he walked up the stairs. Two steps from the top Fr. Fred collapsed and died.

*

A period of three weeks passed by before Josh and Andy, after they had fully recovered from their injuries sustained in the accident and had been discharged from hospital, decided to visit Fr. Fred in his church quarters. When they knocked on the door of the parish house it was opened by another priest, who introduced himself as Fr. John.

"May I help you?" he asked them politely.

"Yes, we have come to see Fr. Fred", they replied.

"I'm afraid Fr. Fred is no longer with us", said Fr. John.

"Oh, where has he gone?" Josh queried.

"Have you not heard?" responded Fr. John.

"Heard what?" asked Josh.

"Fr. Fred died over two weeks ago and was buried in the local cemetery only last week",

"How did he die?" they both asked simultaneously, feeling absolutely shocked by the news.

"Well, before he left he told the church helper, Roy Gross, whose turn it was to lock the church that night, that he was going to visit two young friends of his who were in hospital. His body was found two steps from the top of the staircase alongside which they found no briefcase, wallet or anything else, except a brown paper bag full of white grapes. He had collapsed and died of a heart attack", explained Fr. John.

Josh and Andy were shocked, saddened and devastated to hear such terrible news and tears started running down their cheeks. They thanked Fr. John for explaining what had happened to Fr. Fred and bid him goodnight. On their way home they decided that they would visit Fr. Fred's grave the next day to pay their respects. They realized, rather sorrowfully, that the grapes were intended for them.

During their lunch break the following day, as planned they visited Fr. Fred's grave. There were only two small bunches of flowers that had been placed on it—one from St. Xavier's Church and one from Roy Gross and family—to which they added the bunch of flowers they had taken with them. At the head of the grave was a small, roughly made wooden cross bearing the words:

The Reverend Fr. Fred Cooper
Aged 83
RIP

That was all—nothing else. They felt that the man had no family or longstanding true friends. They both, very sadly, stood at the graveside and thanked him for his forgiveness, friendship and sound advice with regard to their own lives.

They solemnly pledged that they would never let him down. They also promised that, when their funds allowed, they would pay for and have a suitable tombstone erected on his grave. This would then be their way of saying thank you and repaying his kindness and friendship as they realized that the St. Xavier parishioners would not be able to afford such a memorial to this kind, caring, gentle man.

Andy turned to Josh and said, "Hey, Josh, do you remember Fr. Fred's last words to us when we last met him?"

"Yes, I do Andy, yes, I do. They were very poignant words so far as we were concerned", replied Josh.

Fr. Fred's last words to them were:

If we are facing in the right direction
All we have to do is keep walking.
Buddha

Before leaving the priest's graveside the two lads simultaneously quietly said, *'God bless you Fr. Fred and may you rest in peace in God's loving care'*.

THE END

These days there seems to be two words missing from the English language, namely 'PLEASE' and 'THANK YOU', as individuals rarely utter these words, but Josh and Andy did not forget so to do and no doubt Fr. Fred would have been glad as he knew there was a good deal of goodness in the lads.